Mrs. Sifford had been taken to the medical examiner's office. It had been necessary for Mr. Fox, her lawyer, to go there and look at the body and formally swear that this was indeed Mrs. Sifford. On the steel slab, he had seen the face of a determined woman. Her teeth were set tight against death. She was ninety-four and had been fighting death down to the last minute. Why? Why wasn't she glad it was finally over? Fox wondered. Or was it just that she had always been fierce? He knew this much: she had been secretive, assertive, and eccentric. She had hidden things from her family, her bankers, and lawyers. Now she was dead, and still hiding things...

Novels by John Jay Osborn, Jr.

THE PAPER CHASE

THE MAN WHO OWNED NEW YORK

Published by
WARNER BOOKS

The Man Who Owned New York

John Jay Osborn, Jr.

WARNER BOOKS

A Warner Communications Company

The author is grateful for permission to quote from the following sources:

"The Ballad of the Harp-Weaver" from *Collected Poems* by Edna St. Vincent Millay (Harper & Row) **Copyright 1923, 1951** by Edna St. Vincent Millay and Norma Millay Ellis. Reprinted by permission of Norma Millay Ellis. "The Highwayman" from *Collected Poems* by Alfred Noyes. **Copyright 1934** by Alfred Noyes. Reprinted by permission of Harper & Row, Publishers, Inc.

WARNER BOOKS EDITION

This Warner Books Edition is published by arrangement with Houghton Mifflin Company
One Beacon Street
Boston, Massachusetts 02107

Warner Books, Inc.
666 Fifth Avenue
New York, N.Y. 10103

 A Warner Communications Company

Printed in the United States of America

First Warner Books Printing: *May, 1984*

10 9 8 7 6 5 4 3 2 1

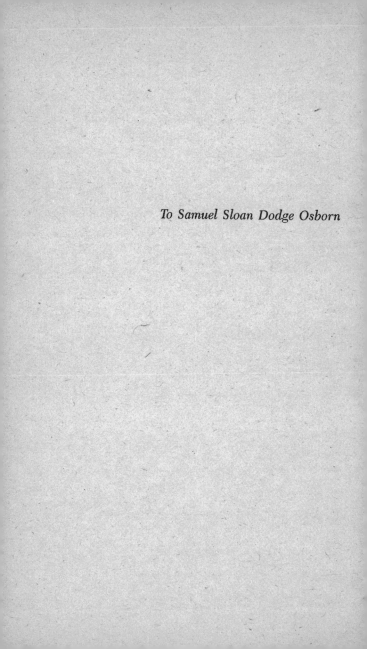

To Samuel Sloan Dodge Osborn

"Nobody owns anything anymore."
—*Kimberly Ashland Hartman*

CONTENTS

PROLOGUE

The thief came in the middle of the night to the Sifford town house on East Seventy-first Street, and defeated the burglar alarm. He used the ornate stone gargoyles as a ladder, and broke in through a third-story window of the narrow five-story house. He was proud of himself. He could feel the silver: there would be lots of it. Then the lights went on and the guard hired by the lawyer Robert Fox leveled a shotgun on the fast boy. The guard was bored and mean: he used the shotgun as a club, which was against Mr. Fox's instructions. Then the guard let the boy go. That was correct: it was good advertising.

All over New York, thieves check the obituaries, talk to each other, and try to get to the stuff while the body is still hot and no one is in the house. The papers had reported that Mrs. Sifford was ninety-four. There might be a maid . . . but what was a maid?

A long time ago, Fox had been taught to place guards at the same time he placed the obituaries. Now, since the thieves paid off the hospital employees, he put them in earlier. The guard had been assigned to the town house when Mrs. Sifford went into the hospital, where she had died on the operating table.

Mrs. Belinda Meecham Sifford's father, "Baron" Meecham, had owned the New York Central. There was a Meecham Park in Brooklyn, which had once been his grandfather's farm, and a Meecham Building, in midtown Manhattan, the building that old Baron Meecham had left to Belinda, his only child, along with seven hundred thousand dollars a year from the Meecham trust funds, as well as the family estate up the Hudson River.

The computers in the New York Trust Company churned out all the figures on Mrs. Sifford's accounts showing how the money had come in and gone out and the bills that had been paid, all clearly listed in black and white. The whole process took only a few hours because most of the records were now on computer discs. The computers of the Walcott brokerage house at Fifteen Wall Street churned out the stock market history of Belinda Meecham Sifford, and a messenger ran the print-outs over to the law firm of Castle and Lovett at Thirty-two Wall Street, where Mr. Fox worked. And bankers all over town helped Fox to open her many safe-deposit boxes buried deep in the vaults of Manhattan. Then the people who had sold her little odds and ends (brokers, insurance people, real estate operators) sent their records over, too, adding to the records Fox already had on file at his firm.

Mrs. Sifford had outlived a great many lawyers, but she had always stayed with one New York law firm, Castle and Lovett, teasing, haranguing, and complaining—especially to Mr. Fox, because he was a "mere boy"—but never leaving. Mr. Fox was thirty-six, but a "boy" to Mrs. Sifford nevertheless.

She had been taken to the medical examiner's office. It had been necessary for Mr. Fox to go there and look at the body and formally swear that this was indeed Mrs. Sifford. On the steel slab, he had seen the face of a determined woman. Her teeth were set tight against death. She was ninety-four and had been fighting death down to the last minute. Why? Why wasn't she glad it was finally over? Fox wondered. Or was it just that she had always been fierce? He knew this much: she had been secretive, assertive, and eccentric. She had hidden things from her family, her bankers, and lawyers. Now she was dead, and still hiding things. Hiding them from her lawyer, who was supposed to assemble all the accumulation of ninety-four years and present it to a judge for approval and then cut it up and distribute it according to the explicit, eccentric instructions that Mrs. Sifford had left in her will.

She had been born in a city that smelled of the horses that plied up and down Fifth Avenue; she had died in a city with the loaded smell of gasoline. That was what she had told Mr. Fox. She claimed that now when you lit a match in the city you could see it burning the air around it. That had been how she felt about New York City in her ninety-fifth year. At least you could see the horse filth and avoid it, she told Mr. Fox. Now, the filth was in the air and ready to explode.

The
Man
Who
Owned
New
York

PART ONE

A River of Gold

THE LAWYER ROBERT FOX was into meditation. He did not call it that, but the fact was that he spent a good deal of his time staring out the window. It was not that he was lazy: at thirty-six, Fox was a partner in a large Wall Street law firm and today anyone has to work hard for that. And it was not because he had no work to do. There was plenty of work, perhaps too much. Robert Fox was into meditation for more practical reasons: he was losing his mind.

He did not realize it, but the deep secrets locked tight in his brain were suddenly and seriously beginning to make noises. There were many reasons for this, none of which Fox comprehended. Instead, he stared out the window trying to keep under control. Unfortunately, he did not even realize that he was staring, meditating, in order to control himself. All he was aware of at this particular point was the daily movement of the events in his life. When something came up, he dealt with it. When it didn't, he stared out the window.

Today, he saw the sky over Manhattan turn pale red, then blue, and the clouds lowered. The underbelly of the sky went dark red again, like a huge ceiling lit by the lights of the city. Finally, the office buildings dissolved too in the night mist, so that the red ceiling sky seemed dangerously unsupported.

"Excuse me."

Something had come up, and Fox turned away from the window. A young associate lawyer stood in the door. Fox nodded at the dark figure, dressed in a gray suit and blue tie striped with red, each hair on his head lying obediently in place.

"Yes, Jackson," Fox said.

"You asked for a status report on Mrs. Sifford's papers."

"And?"

"I've been looking through them, concentrating on October nineteen sixty-seven. Trying to find out who her friends were. Her servants. I've been trying to find the private payroll, as you instructed. Unfortunately, sir, I have nothing to report."

"What's the problem?" Fox said wearily.

Fox was kneading his aching shoulders. Jackson stood ramrod straight. He looked so polished that, to Fox, the young lawyer seemed to shine. Does he use a sun lamp to get that tan? Fox wondered. Is that why he shines?

"The problem is the warehouse, sir. The electricity goes off and on. The problem is that there are over forty-four dusty, mildewed cardboard boxes of papers, arranged in no particular order. I've been reading by flashlight as the rats run under my feet."

Fox stood up behind his desk. He stretched. Fox was tall, thin, rumpled. There were black circles under his eyes, because he had not been sleeping well. Even so, Robert Fox looked powerful and handsome.

"I apologize for the fact that not everything in the world is on computer tape, Jackson. I apologize for the fact I have to have a lawyer on this job and can't send a paraprofessional. There are a lot of boxes because Mrs. Sifford lived for a very long time. She had to store her papers somewhere."

"Sir, you asked me to concentrate on nineteen sixty-seven. The papers for that year are a complete mess."

"Just keep digging away like a good little mole."

It's late, Fox thought. Got to get moving toward home. He put on his coat. When he looked up, Jackson was still in his office.

"Is there more, Jackson?"

"My personal status evaluation, sir."

Jackson was a second-year associate lawyer. Every six months all the young lawyers were given reports by the partners they had been working with. The reports were a sort of grade and a pat on the back.

"Jackson, your work has been perfect," Fox snapped.

"Thank you."

"You look perfect. Your work is perfect. You're one of the best young lawyers I've ever seen, but that shouldn't surprise you, should it?"

"Thank you," Jackson said again.

"As far as I can see you've never done anything wrong. But you know that, don't you. You've read your own résumé, I presume. For you it's all been straight up, like some young rocket going off the launch pad at Cape Kennedy. Exeter, Harvard College, Harvard Law School, *Harvard Law Review*. A, A, A. Perfect. You know it and I know it. So don't pretend you need me to tell you that. I'm sure you've got plenty of plans for the future. I'm sure you're planning to marry the daughter of the president of one of our corporate clients, and that you're working for the election of some senator in your spare time."

"Spare time?"

Maybe Jackson does have a sense of humor, Fox thought, and then thought better of it. No, it must have been a slip.

"Listen," Fox said, "I apologize, but I can't talk to you all night. If I've been rude, I apologize for that, too. Even young partners like me have their ups and downs. We get frozen, Jackson."

Fox stopped in midsentence. Was he going to see Kim Hartman tonight? No. So it was a frozen dinner. He had to get rid of Jackson.

"I know I'm cranky, Jackson. All I can say is that I'm thirty-six, and *I'm* not going anywhere. I'm not young and strapped to a rocket. This is where I stay. At this firm, at this desk. I'm sort of in a time vault. Understand?"

"Not really, sir."

"Frozen, Jackson. But from my time vault position, I get a good look at the young rockets that shoot past. Your report is excellent. You are a credit to this firm. When you leave to take a better job, I will give you a letter of recommendation. That's your status report, Jackson. Now back to your stinking warehouse."

Fox yawned.

"We're finished?" Jackson asked.

Were they, Fox wondered? No, he had forgotten something. Fox spun and suddenly stuck out his hand. It was a big, strong hand, and Fox rammed it at Jackson like a karate chop. Jackson jumped back.

"Jackson," Fox muttered, "it's just a hand. Not some strange bird flying around this office. Just a little hand." Fox stretched his hand toward Jackson. "Congratulations on your evaluation," Fox thundered. "Shake!"

Slowly, delicately, and with extreme caution, Jackson shook the strange bird's hand.

2

IT WAS TIME TO go home, but since Fox was not seeing Kim Hartman this night, it took him awhile to get moving. He did not want to face his own apartment and the things in it. Everything was much, much nicer at Kim Hartman's, even though she had decorated her place in a very peculiar way. But Fox did move because of Gauder. The old man had taught Fox how to be a lawyer, and now that Gauder had retired, Fox took him home when possible.

It was late now and even the hard-working young associate lawyers had cleared out of the firm. Fox passed covered typewriters on the secretaries' desks in the hallway and thought the black plastic typewriter covers looked like body bags for babies. He moved faster toward Gauder.

He had a way to go: Gauder's office was tucked in the far reaches of the firm. No corner office now, just one window, and the old huge desk, which took up most of the space. Gauder was not even "of counsel" to the firm anymore. The young lawyers sometimes mistook him for an old messenger, as he carefully slid along the floor, one foot at a time, sometimes with a hand on the wall to support him. Gauder was a beast that now existed only with the help of the elevator system, the taxicab, and the nice doorman. There was no one left for him now and damn few places for him to go. Fox wondered if anyone else remembered what Gauder had been.

This is what I am to become, Fox thought, when it is all said and done. Except that by the time I'm Gauder's age, if I live to be Gauder's age, the fast boys of today will be in charge, and they will not even allow me a closet where I can turn the yellowed sheets and remember the deals I once made. We have a pension plan now, he thought, they tell you to retire at sixty-five. I voted for that, didn't I? What was I thinking about? The only good pension plan is letting you keep your office.

Gauder's door was open, as it always was, an invitation seldom accepted.

"How are you?" Fox asked.

Gauder's thin hands, with long blue veins, lay on

top of the paper he was studying. His eyes were two inches from the sheet. The bald head and thin neck were draped with folds of parchment skin. The shoulders poked like rods up through his charcoal gray suit.

"Yes?" Gauder said. "Who?"

"Fox, sir."

"Oh, Fox," Gauder said. "Yes, we'll get it all back now."

"What, sir?" Fox said.

"Why, the bonds, Fox, the China bonds. Now we'll show them."

The old man's eyes blinked as he talked and began the slow process of rising from his desk, pushing himself up.

"They thought we'd never see the day and now we will, you can bet on it. The China bonds."

"What China bonds?" Fox asked.

"Damn it, the China bonds, loans to China. When there was an emperor and all that. Fox, did you know that China money has a hole in the center of it? I'm talking about the metal money. A hole. I wrote China bonds. Then there wasn't any China anymore, Fox, just a bunch of red devils marching over the place, and no money. They wouldn't pay the bonds. They repudiated them!"

"This arm," Fox said. He was holding Gauder's coat for him, and the old man was trying to stick his left arm in the right sleeve. Fox got him turned the right way, finally, and found the cane.

"When the Chinks repudiated, everyone on the Street papered their walls with the China bonds," Gauder babbled. "They flew them out the windows here on the Street. Flew them out like aeroplanes or ticker tape. But I've got mine. Now we don't call them Reds. They're Chinas once more, and Fox, this new Chink, Chairman Hua, says they're going to pay the bonds.''

"That's good, sir," Fox said. He turned out the light in Gauder's office and, taking his arm, steered him toward the elevator.

They got into the elevator. The man took them straight down. The marble on the first floor had just been washed and it shone in the blue night. Fox was very careful with the old man, and it took them a long time to cross the big lobby. Gauder's cane went crack, crack on the floor, and Fox paced along at the other arm.

Then they got to the revolving door. This was always the hard part. Fox got Gauder's hunched body into one of the slits. He turned the door for him, delicately, thinking that in the glass slip, Gauder looked like a man pickled in formaldehyde. Fox thought of Lenin's tomb. Lenin was pickled, too. What had the Chinese done with Mao?

Finally, Gauder reached the outside and Fox spun through the door, went out to the curb, and got lucky with a cab. He lowered Gauder in, then he went around the other side and slid in, too. The cab turned on to empty Broadway, then twisted left for the West Side Highway. It was a big, quiet cab. In the yellow light of the back seat, Gauder's eyes seemed to be the biggest thing in his body. They bulged out, blinking constantly.

"Mrs. Sifford had Chinas," Gauder said.

"We've found her bonds," Fox answered.

"Where to?" the cab driver asked.

"Sixty-third and Park," Fox told him.

"Sure thing," the driver said very quietly. This is a lucky night, Fox thought. I got Gauder out of the office, I got him a good cab, and probably he'll get up to his apartment all right and won't die tonight. And he'll probably come in tomorrow and go to work on his China bonds. Why not? Fox thought. Let him damn well work on his bonds and old papers forever. Screw the fast boys like Jackson. I like these slow-moving old bats. You never know what they're going to say. With the others, all you get is a reflection of your own mind.

"I know you've got trouble with Mrs. Sifford," Gauder said suddenly. "Everyone had trouble with her. First she was all over the city, ordering everyone around. Telling people to clean up the place and whatnot. Then she hid in her town house, and nobody could reach her."

The cab swung slowly off the highway, cut through Central Park, and then went into the East Side. Insulated from the city, Fox felt the beauty of it. Here in Midtown everything was moving in a slow dance of lights.

"Well?" Gauder said.

"Excuse me?"

"Well, why keep it from me? Why can't I know?"

"Keep what from you?" Fox asked.

"The trouble with Mrs. Sifford," and he squeezed Fox's hand so hard that the nails dug in. Fox thought of acupuncture and thought, too: The old man has got me worrying about the Chinese, and now I'll want Chinese food, not a frozen dinner. What is it? The year of the snake? The leopard? Maybe it's the year of the wolf.

"Thirteen years ago, Mrs. Sifford walked into a strange bank and mortgaged the Meecham Building. The interest was paid regularly. But the money, the equity, is gone. No trace of it."

Gauder's head bobbed.

"Really, Fox," he said, "are you sure? How much money?"

"Three million two hundred thousand dollars. I'm really sure. I checked the bank out myself."

"How interesting," Gauder said. "I wonder what she did with the money. I'll think about it. I'll help you, Fox."

The cab stopped in front of the awning at Five ninety-eight Park Avenue, and the doorman came out. He reached in for Gauder, and slowly and carefully pulled the old man from the cab. Fox handed the cane out the window.

"Ask Gladney," Gauder said over his shoulder. "He ought to know something."

"Good night," Fox yelled back.

"Where to now?" the cab driver asked.

"Around the block to the Wong Too Szechuan Palace."

3

THE TELEPHONE WAS ringing. It had its own particular sound. The old kind: a powerful kicking ring that seemed to command Fox to answer it. He put his briefcase between his knees and struggled with the old bronze lock that had never worked right. Finally, he managed to click the tumbler and the door swung open. Fox got the key out of the lock, his briefcase under his shoulder, and flicked on the lights.

The small lights that lined the long hallway had little faded curtains around them. It wasn't much light. This was an old apartment, inherited by Fox from his father, and nothing had been changed.

The ringing of the telephone was loud now that he was in the hall. He headed for it, striding fast down the frayed red carpet, toward the telephone room. He dropped the briefcase in the hall and pulled open the door. The light went on as the door opened and, as his hand reached the receiver, the ringing stopped. He picked up the receiver anyway.

This damn phone has never worked right, Fox thought. He listened to the buzz of the empty line. It was an old black square phone, and the cords were covered in stitched cotton, not plastic. It sat on its table in the little telephone room looking solid and

13

respectable. Kim Hartman has recessed telephones hidden all over her apartment, Fox thought. And they don't ring, they hum. At the law firm, we've got a damn system with so many lights and buzzers no one can understand it. I've got this. He stared at the old phone. Who called me? he wondered. If I had an answering machine, maybe I would know. Kim Hartman has an answering machine.

The telephone room was bigger than a phone booth, but not by much. Fox had the door to it open, and his feet stuck out into the hall. He put the receiver back on its cradle and just sat there, sort of resting. Had it been Kim Hartman on the line? He looked at the phone: Tell me, he thought.

And then, in a strange way, the phone did seem to tell him something. A memory seemed to ruffle through Fox's mind like wind on water. It was there, and then it was gone. Did I forget something, something at the office? he wondered. The memory came again. It seemed to sail through his mind, invisible but tangible. He could *feel* it, but he could not remember it. It doesn't matter, he decided finally. It all gets evened out in the next world.

Fox got up and picked up his briefcase from the hall and took it into the kitchen. It was a big room, with a large white table in the center and a fan and light in the ceiling over the table. He put his briefcase down on the table and got Scotch and a glass from the cupboard. Did I pick up any plastic forks? he wondered. He couldn't remember, so he opened the silver drawer, and took out a fork.

There was a microwave oven on the counter. It was the only change, the only addition, that Fox had made to the apartment he had inherited. I don't need that tonight, Fox thought, looking at the oven. The Chinese food is still hot. He put down paper towels, opened his briefcase, and pulled out the little white containers. They weren't dripping, but he put them on the paper towels anyway.

The snow peas went well with the Scotch. So did the black mushrooms and bamboo shoots from the Szechuan Palace. Good for Gauder, Fox thought. And he had another drink.

From the window, Fox looked out over a good portion of Midtown. To the south, they had torn down an old building. Fox could see Gauder's apartment house, only two blocks away. He could see the line of traffic spreading in a knit-together pattern of different lights as the cars and buses fought their way down Lexington Avenue. At ten o'clock at night, Midtown was still alive and moving.

I'll call Kim Hartman, Fox thought, what the hell. What was she doing tonight? Why aren't we together?

He had finished eating, and now he folded up all the containers in the paper towels and threw them into the garbage. He tossed the silver fork into the sink. There was a rumbling. Was it the old back elevator lumbering by? They'll tear this place down too, Fox thought. He shut the briefcase and carried it down the hall, into the living room. He threw it on the mahogany coffee table and lay down on the couch with a full glass of Scotch.

It was a black leather couch, old, with cracks now appearing around the bronze knobs that tacked the leather to the frame. Across the room, there was a large painting of Fox's mother. He stared at it, lying on his side, drinking.

His mother was blonde, tall, and young in the painting. He wondered if she had actually been as pretty as the picture made her look. It was a soft painting. The dark eyes seemed to hone in on Fox. It's some sort of trick, Fox thought, all the painters do that. I'll ask Kim about it.

He got up to call her.

It took a long time before he got a dial tone. Waiting for it, the little flutter went through his brain. It was a message all right, poetry, like a nursery rhyme. How did it go?

> There sat my mother
> With the harp against her shoulder,
> Looking nineteen,
> And not a day older

The poetry just popped up in his brain. All sorts of strange things are popping up lately, he thought. Who taught me that? My mother? He looked at the black telephone. He had the dial tone and he used it. The rotary dial clicked back as he dialed. And then it began to ring.

I'm not going to reach Kim Hartman, Fox thought, not on this telephone. Why is it that I feel as if I can never reach anyone on this goddamned old phone? I have always felt that way, and it is true. This phone does not work. It did work, though. Fox could hear it ring. Kim Hartman just wasn't home. He put down the receiver.

You don't reach people on this old phone unless it wants you to reach them, Fox thought, angrily, irrationally, blaming the fact that Kim Hartman was out on the telephone he had inherited from his father. He took a long pull on the glass of Scotch. I've got to get rid of his old junk. I've got to get some extensions.

> A smile about her lips,
> And a light about her head,
> And her hands in the harp-strings
> Frozen dead.

He had been cursing at the telephone, and it seemed to shoot the poetry back at him, as if it were a dream phone that talked without ringing, talked when it wanted, and sent him strange messages from the past that he could neither decipher nor stop.

4

THE OLD CUT-GLASS chandelier twirled slowly in the breeze from the new air-conditioning system.

"I remember old Mr. Sifford very well, Fox," Frederick Gladney said. "He was a big tall man, bald, red-faced from drinking. Always asking for money. His wife's money."

The chandelier had more or less hypnotized Fox and it was difficult for him to pull his eyes away and look at Gladney.

"How do you like the wine?" Gladney said.

"Fine."

The wine cellars of the New York Trust Company were the best in the city. And a special wine steward, dressed in a black coat, had come to the private dining room and formally presented the bottle of vintage Simi to Gladney and Fox before lunch.

"I'm old, Fox," Gladney went on, "but not old enough to have been around when she married him. I don't know why she did it. I can only guess. I think she wanted to reform him. Mrs. Sifford was religious and rich, and used to think she could reform the world. Charles Sifford was ten years younger than his wife, but he looked older, because of the drink."

"When did he leave?" Fox asked.

"I don't know exactly. She didn't tell me anything. I was just her banker. His account is still at the bank. But it's been inactive for thirteen years. For a while, I thought he was on vacation. Then I thought he'd left her. Or she'd thrown him out when she finally realized he wasn't going to change. Then, Fox, for a long time, I fantasized that he was dead and probably buried down in the cellar of the town house. Finally, I just gave up thinking about it. I don't know what I think. Are you absolutely sure that Mrs. Sifford mortgaged the Meecham Building?"

"Yes," Fox said. "She walked into another bank on a day in October, thirteen years ago, took three million in equity out of the building. Besides that, her son cosigned the mortgage papers. I'm sure."

"Old people," Gladney sighed. "You can't tell what they'll do. They get secretive and scared. Maybe she bought diamonds. Put them in her safe-deposit box."

"We've opened her boxes," Fox said. "She had a lot of them, but no diamonds."

"Then maybe she did buy her husband off. Gave him three million dollars in pocket money and told him to take off for Rio. Who knows? He was a strong man. He'd only be about eighty now. Maybe he'll come back and start using his checking account. Who have you told about this?"

Gladney was about sixty. He wore a double-breasted old-style blue suit, and a white handkerchief was carefully arranged so that it issued in points from his breast pocket. He dresses the way he did when he started banking, Fox thought. Just the way he did forty years ago, when he began working on the Meecham and Sifford accounts.

"I haven't told anybody at your bank."

"Thank you," Gladney said. "But they'll find out anyway. The rumors will begin. And they'll say it casts suspicion on me, and fire me. They're looking for any excuse."

"They don't need to know for a while."

They were the new board of directors of the New York Trust Company. Frederick Gladney had not changed in forty years, but the bank had.

"You can't protect me," Gladney said. "It doesn't matter."

"It matters to me," Fox said quietly.

Seventy years ago, when Mrs. Sifford began banking with the New York Trust Company, it had been a "ladies" bank. Powerful, secure in a stone building that looked like a club. Dealing with old money. Now it was "macho." Things are changing, Fox thought. At the moment, down in the lobby, construction

19

people were putting the final touches on a decorating scheme that emphasized circular black Formica desks, chrome chairs, black leather. They were also putting in a new floor that looked to Fox like tire tread, but was probably made in Italy and costing the bank a million dollars a square foot. This old chandelier will go too, Fox thought.

"I saw the TV ad where your new president stands on top of an office building wearing a hard hat and appears to field rivets with his bare hands, yelling, 'Trust New York Trust. We get our hands dirty for you.' What's next, Frederick?"

"I predict that our idiot leader will jump from a jet, in a three-piece suit, parachute strapped to his back, hard hat in place: 'New York Trust, where the president is only a free fall away.'"

Fox laughed. He liked Gladney because he wouldn't change. He had become Gladney's friend because he was one of the few bankers in New York with a sense of humor.

"So you think the money went with Mr. Sifford?"

"Probably."

"And you actually think there's a chance he'll come back?"

"Anything is possible."

"If you were I, what would you do?"

Gladney looked up at the twirling glass.

"I don't know, Fox. As executor of the estate, your law firm has to follow certain rules. I don't know. You'll search the records, copy all the papers, uncover all the bodies, and do it quietly. I know you. It's not what I want, but it's what you'll do."

"What do you want?"

Gladney stopped staring at the ceiling and the chandelier. His blue eyes bore in on Fox, pleading.

"I want you to say there is an accounting error in the estate. Declare old Mr. Sifford legally dead. Forget the whole thing. Give me time to get my gold watch and retire with a pension. I was her banker. I'm supposed to watch over her money, know what she did. More than three million dollars has disappeared? When Mrs. Sifford died, she handed me a death ticket too."

"But you didn't do anything," Fox said. "You couldn't stop her from secretly going to another bank. Or not telling anyone what happened to her husband. Or giving him three million to get him out of her life."

"I know I didn't do anything," Gladney said, his voice rising. "That is just what they are going to say. 'Why didn't you do something, Mr. Gladney. *Why?*'"

Why indeed? Fox asked himself.

5

"YES, ALGUR," Fox said.

Miss Algur, Fox's secretary, liked things to run smoothly. Her principal preoccupations were typing and dusting.

"It's *Miss* Algur, *Mr.* Fox. Please get that straight."

According to Miss Algur, Fox was acting, lately, a little "loose." She was trying to make him snap out of it.

"You have another Mr. Sifford in the waiting room," she said. And rolled her eyes at the ceiling.

"Send him to Jackson."

"*Mr.* Jackson is in the warehouse. Has been for a week."

"All right, *Miss* Algur, I'll take him myself. What's the status report from the receptionist?"

"A mumbler," Miss Algur said, and stamped out.

You can turn them away, Fox thought, but then they just wait for you in the elevator or down on the street, ready to jump you, with their frayed, parched papers. So you've got to see them. It is the only way to close off the matter. It's what Gauder always did when he had lunatic trouble.

Fox stood up politely when the lunatic came in. He had a puffy, lined red face and eyes that matched, so that it was very hard to tell his age. You could smell the thick scent of mouthwash to cover up, and the suit was newly pressed, but did not fit right. It reminded Fox for some reason of the ill-fitting suit that he had worn to a fancy dance many years ago, when he had wanted to look like a certain thing he was not, and had failed.

"Please sit down, Mr. Sifford," Fox said.

"And I *am* Mr. Sifford," the red-faced man mumbled. "I know you don't believe me or you wouldn't have kept me waiting out there in your goddamned anteroom for three hours. You don't believe me, but it's the damn truth. I couldn't come back until she died."

"Of course," Fox said.

"I couldn't," he said. "She told me not to."

"Yes," Fox said, and thought, how easy it was to get clients here in New York. All those people who walk the streets mumbling are potential clients, rehearsing their cases. All of them are ready with aged deeds, yellowed pieces of paper with pencil marks on them, or sometimes they bring descriptions of inventions: "You know the telephone. I really invented it, not Bell." They come with newspaper clippings and genealogies.

Fox had begun to realize that someone was stealing lives all over New York. They even came with pictures: "They stole my face," the model tells you. "My face is up now over Times Square, and it's stolen. It was my look. They took it off the photograph I left with the agency. I tell you it's my face. Look at me: you tell me." And then you look at the face. Sometimes it was a nice face, but the body of the girl was usually thin from not eating, too damn thin, and Fox always wanted to give her money to eat. They had stolen her face: what can you do about it? What can you tell them? That someone is stealing lives all over town, stealing brains, and turning them crazy?

"Ask me the questions," the man snapped.

"What questions?" Fox said.

"You've got some sort of test," he said.

"There isn't any test," Fox said.

"Then just give me my money." The man's red eyes bulged out now at Fox, like the bulging eyes of a dead fish left too long in the sun. Who knows what the man really believes, Fox thought. Who can actually tell? Probably he actually does believe that he's the long-lost husband of Belinda Meecham Sifford. They carry the faded newspaper clippings around so long that before the paper disintegrates the lines are permanently embedded into their brains.

"I've had a rough time," the man said, "ever since she threw me out. I've been through a lot. It's my turn now."

Gladney had reported that in his seventies Mr. Sifford had been easily six four, a strapping man. If this was Mr. Sifford, he'd shortened a lot over the years. Then there was the hair. In his thirteen missing years, the bald Mr. Sifford seemed to have grown a full head of red hair. What do you say to them? Fox wondered. How do you deal with the mumblers: the Rumanian princes, the great inventors, the spectacular artists, the heirs, the owners, the musicians? Life is tough all over, Fox thought, and get drunk enough for long enough, let your life be just tough enough, and you just goddamn become someone else. You say you're Napoleon, and they lock you up in Bellevue.

"I've got bad news," Fox said.

"What?" the man said.

"She wrote you out of the will." In fact it was the truth. Belinda Meecham Sifford had left not one cent to her husband. He only retained certain trust rights created when they had married. Mrs. Sifford couldn't change that. Maybe he had known that. Maybe that was why he deserted her and never came back.

"Liar," the red-faced man yelled.

"Here's the will," Fox said. He pulled it out,

pushed it across the desk. But the man didn't touch it.

"Liar," he said again, then, "bitch."

"Horrible," Fox said.

"The bitch," the man snapped, and now began wobbling, side to side. "Not one cent. Bitch. Liar. And all these years with no money, waiting for her to die, and not one cent. Help me."

"What can I do?" Fox said.

"Contest the will," he screamed.

"I can't," Fox told him. "I represent the estate. You need another lawyer for that."

The man got up slowly and began mumbling. He was mumbling about his bitch wife, and telling himself that he would get another lawyer. He would find a good one. You did not wait thirteen years and give up now. He would prove his case. Fox stood up to see him out. Sometimes they sit in the back of courtrooms, and that's enough for them, Fox thought, just being spectators. Sometimes they go over the line. Here in New York too many have gone over the line. He'll try to find another lawyer all right, Fox thought. He'll go from elevator to elevator and floor to floor, waiting for someone to give him the test, and take the case. There are so many of them out in this city, do they do any harm? Only when they want to kill you.

Then Fox called the true heir to the Sifford estate. Mrs. Sifford's son, Charles Sifford, Jr.

6

FOX DIALED THE call himself, and the phone rang for a long time before it was answered. Charles Sifford, Jr., sounded like he'd run a long way to get to it.

"Yes?" he panted.

"It's Robert Fox, calling about your mother's estate."

"Yes, Mr. Fox. I thought that was through. Didn't I sign some papers?"

Yes, Fox thought, you signed some papers. A month ago. And thirteen years ago, too.

"I was wondering if you plan to be in New York again," Fox said. "There are some more things to sign, and I would like to get some instructions on several matters."

"I don't know," Mr. Sifford said. "Come back to the city? Again?"

"That's right," Fox said.

"I just don't know."

Mr. Sifford seemed confused by the questions. Did he plan to be in the city? Did he plan anything?

"Please wait a minute. Is that all right?"

"Certainly." Fox waited and then his wife came on the line.

"What's this all about?"

The voice was very clear and direct. It reminded Fox of something. You begin to recognize a certain tone that means banker, a style that says lawyer. This woman had a tone that meant something and set off a ringing in Fox's own telephone brain, but when he tried to plug her voice into a connection, his memory bank went dead.

"I was wondering if your husband and you might possibly be coming to the city, so that we could meet and he could sign some more papers, as well as issue me some instructions as the principal beneficiary of his mother's estate."

"He does not plan to be in New York," Mrs. Sifford said. "The funeral was too much."

"I see."

"You're a lawyer, aren't you, Mr. Fox. You get paid for all this. Why don't you plan to be here?"

She said all this in a particular professional tone that was somehow soothing, so that Fox didn't really mind that he was being issued an order. And why not issue an order? he thought. They are the damned clients.

"Of course, I could arrange to visit you."

As soon as he said it, a plan began to shape. Kim Hartman. Yes, he might love to visit.

"Would it be inconvenient if I came on a weekend?" Fox asked.

"Every day is the same to us here," she said. "So it doesn't matter when you come, except that my husband takes a nap between two and four. Come with your papers anytime you want, but come in the morning. Good-bye, Mr. Fox."

She didn't give him a chance to say good-bye, but

27

again, she was not rude. It was all in the way she had said good-bye, so that it didn't require an answer from anyone. It was a definite style all right, a particular type of person, someone trained a long time to do things in a certain way, trained so deeply that she could not shake it.

"Mr. Fox," Miss Algur said from the door, "you have an appointment at the Sifford town house, with Mrs. Hartman, which you have apparently forgotten."

Algur had to dodge: Fox grabbed his coat, flew past her.

7

IT WAS FALL, and the weather was unpredictable. The sky did not seem to know what to do. To the east there were huge clouds, piled up, black and bulging. But here it was sunny, cool. Even Fox felt it: it was good to be outside. The street was tree lined and lovely. Then the yellow cab came, and Fox thought: the hell with the weather, and started down the steps.

From the corner of their eyes, two ladies walking tiny dogs stopped and watched Kim Hartman get out of the cab. They knew that they had not looked that good at forty, and they realized too that Kim Hartman did not mind people knowing she was forty. She had inherited the look, and the bones, gestures, and manner of talking that went with it. She was tall, thin, blonde, and her hair was pulled back just enough to show her pearl earrings; there was just enough lipstick so that the women saw that her mouth was perfect. They yanked their dogs away from her.

Watching Kim, Fox thought about the other part of her inheritance, the black part of her mind, handed down to her by a long list of forebears who had ended up stepping out the windows of office buildings, vegetating in sanatoriums in Richmond, or drinking themselves to death over backgammon tables. What kind of mood would Kim be in today?

"Good morning, briefcase brain," Kim Hartman said. She reached up, put her long fingers on Fox's cheek, and kissed him. He was still absorbing "briefcase brain" as Kim Hartman stepped back, a hand up shielding her eyes from the sun while she inspected the house.

The buildings on the left and right had plain modern facades. The Sifford town house was baroque, with stone carvings of grotesque laughing faces, deeply etched pillars around the windows, intricate lintels and cornices. The sunlight seemed to get lost, shooting into crevices. In all the windows, the curtains were drawn. The city soot of sixty years had given the stone a black patina.

"I don't want the job," Kim said.

"You haven't even looked inside."

"I just don't like the feeling."

Kim Hartman was an artist and an art appraiser. She felt things. And generally she acted the way she felt.

"Come and look," Fox said. "It can't hurt you."

She gave Fox a look that implied she was certainly not sure about that. But she let Fox take her arm and lead her up the steps. Fox's key clicked the solid tumblers and they were in the foyer, looking for the light switch.

"Is there a guard?" Kim asked.

"Upstairs," Fox told her, and found the switch.

It was old-time, subdued lighting, the kind Fox had in his own apartment. To the left, a dark mahogany staircase swept up in a spiral. To the right, there was a hall lined with pictures, each with a little brass label and a light over it. The floor was black marble. At the end of the hall there were three doors and a chair covered with a sheet. The place smelled musty.

"You say no one's living here?" Kim said.

"Mrs. Sifford was the last of her kind. Her son lives in the country."

"I don't know, Fox," she said. "I just don't know. What's wrong with the estate?"

"A few accounting problems."

"A few accounting problems?" she said. "There's a lot more wrong than that. I can tell that much just standing here. I feel ghosts."

"Just come and look at the place."

Kim took off her raincoat and threw it on the banister. She shook her head, but they started down the hall, looking at the pictures as they went.

When they came to the doors at the end of the hall, she stopped, sat down on the draped chair, without even bothering to pull off the sheet and check to see if it was a delicate French antique that might collapse under her.

"We've just passed about three hundred thousand

30

dollars worth of American art, Fox," she said wearily. "This is the kind of house where even the bathroom fixtures would have to be catalogued. Do you know how much time this estate appraisal will take? Do you know how much I'll have to charge?"

They went into the living room. Fox pulled the covers off a blue sofa held up by a carved spiral lattice designed to look as if the sofa legs didn't touch the ground. Kim Hartman leaned against Fox and he put his arm around her.

"No, Fox," she said quietly. "I love you, but I won't do this job. It doesn't feel right."

Then she saw the painting. It was enormous: taking up most of the wall. Four huge mountains rose up into a sky blazing in a golden sunset. The Hudson River cut through the mountains, looking muscular as it twisted through the gorge, as if it was running toward something important. In the foreground there was a mansion of spectacular dimensions.

"I've had a bad week," Kim said, holding Fox's hand. "I got the curse in a white dress on Fifth Avenue. I found cocaine in Robert's room. I believe his father gave it to him on their last weekend together. Now this."

"What?" Fox asked.

"This painting. It is by Frederick Edwin Church, probably painted around eighteen ninety. It's worth approximately seven hundred and fifty thousand dollars. It is also a work of art. I love it. All right. I'll take the job, Fox, if you promise to handle the ghosts."

They went out again into the street to look for a cab. Kim Hartman was holding Fox's arm. It felt awfully good to have her hold his arm and to be walking around New York with her. To Fox, it felt like three million two.

8

THAT EVENING, the fact that Fox's office did not have any photographs suddenly struck him as pathetic. There were reasons for this, of course. How could he hang up a picture of Kim? Now Jackson could hang pictures of his women on the walls. Jackson was twenty-five, and the girls he had pictures of were models, it seemed to Fox, all of them blonde and wonderful.

Jackson is protected by his age, Fox thought, in a way that I'm not. All the people who know me also know Kim and they probably know we're having an affair, but you still didn't advertise it with photographs on your walls. It is not done. What would Gauder say? Or have said when he still had a brain?

Probably nothing. He would have simply stared at the picture and that would have been enough. No photos on my walls, just damned diplomas, old inherited nautical prints. What went wrong? Why do I live a life in which I don't have photos?

Something is definitely happening to my mind, there's a sea change coming, I'm beginning to want things I never thought about before. Is it all because of Kim, or is there more? There was a lot more, but Fox stopped thinking about it.

"Yes, Jackson."

The associate had slipped in through the open door and was standing in his dark suit in front of Fox's desk. How long has he been here? Fox wondered. And why do I feel as if this twenty-five-year-old lawyer can read my mind?

"Sir, I have finally discovered some information."

"Yes?"

"I have found an interesting convection that may relate, in some fashion, to our problem."

Convection? "Just talk, Jackson. Simple English."

"The penthouse apartment at the top of the Sifford town house. Thirteen years ago, it was occupied by one Marsiglia. Now I find that interesting, sir."

Marsiglia? What was Jackson talking about? Why was he standing, waiting, as if he'd delivered an extremely vital piece of information?

"I hate to disappoint you, Jackson, but I've got absolutely no idea what you're blabbering about."

"Marsiglia," Jackson sputtered, "the man who owns New York. *That* Marsiglia."

Now *that* Marsiglia Fox *had* heard of. "The Man Who Owns New York" had been a long article in the *New York Times*. And it was very interesting. Because in about three thousand words it had said very little about Marsiglia, except that it listed some of the properties he supposedly owned. If he did own them, then he had taken control of a lot of New York in just thirteen years. And he didn't want to talk about it.

"What is the convection?" Fox said quietly.

"Sir, Mr. Marsiglia started to acquire his holdings thirteen years ago. At the same time that Mr. Sifford seems to drop out of all the warehouse records, when Mrs. Sifford mortgaged her building, when the money disappeared. Marsiglia lived on top of her. Don't you see?"

"Jackson, I find the phrase 'on top of her' disgusting."

"There's more. I checked the records."

"What records?"

"I thought you would like me to find out about Marsiglia's first venture, the one he started thirteen years ago. The Blagden Building on Park Avenue. His first big deal. I checked the records with the secretary of state. It lists Marsiglia's investors in that project. Well, I found out that all the investors were corporations, most of them now defunct. Because that didn't seem to say much, I checked the records of the corporations themselves and came up with the original incorporators."

Jackson broke character. He seemed to smile for an instant, as if proud of himself. He handed the list of names over to Fox.

"They are all lawyers," Fox said finally. "All young lawyers like you. Except, of course, we'll find out that some of them were office boys, because maybe there weren't enough young lawyers around who they could make the president and vice president, and the secretary of state. Maybe it was a small law firm, in some cases, and some of the lawyers were on vacation. This is how it's done. You set up a corporate vehicle to channel investment money. You want to protect yourself with the corporate rules of limited liability. You want to protect your anonymity. You tell your smart law firm to set up your corporation, and they bring in their smart young men, who are perfectly willing to sign anything put in front of them because they want to make partner. Understand?''

"Yes," Jackson said.

"How many times have you signed a corporate charter that one of our partners slapped down on your desk?"

"A couple," Jackson said.

"Ten years later, Jackson, you won't remember what you signed or who the clients were. Also, these corporations are set up specifically for each specific investment deal, and dissolved after the deal is completed. So they're hard as hell to figure out anyway. The only time you get any kind of real record is when a deal goes badly, and everybody ends up suing everybody. Don't ever sign anything.''

Jackson had listened, but he didn't talk. He had put on his blank, television stare, so that Fox found it impossible to read his mind.

"Listen, Jackson, I'm trying to teach you something. Even in law firms like ours, which are completely honest and everything is wonderful and you get to work for a great guy like me, even here, sometimes things go sour. It turns out that the little venture capital gamble is all crooked. It turns out that the money came from some crook. Ten years later, when you're running for president, Jackson, some smart boy who's trying to make his name in the U.S. attorney's office will be investigating, and will find the corporation, and even though you just signed your name, it's a lot of fun to pull you in before the grand jury. You know what I mean?''

"Yes," Jackson said, "I'm sorry this list isn't any help. I guess it's back to the warehouse."

"Jackson," Fox said, and now *he* smiled, "it is a help. Or may be some help. And I'm very grateful to you for doing the scut work involved in finding this stuff out. One of the lawyers listed here is an old friend of mine."

"So I'm finished?"

"Wrong. It's back to your warehouse, rats, and flashlight. Sorry. But there is a hopeful sign: I'm beginning to like you. In spite of myself."

Fox thought: Why am I taunting him? What's wrong with me? Suddenly he felt a little better about Jackson because he had made Jackson feel vulnerable, or hoped he had. And why is this important to me? he wondered. Because I'm beginning to feel damned vulnerable myself? He lifted his head to try to explain a little of this to Jackson, to at least say something human to him, but Jackson had gone away as quietly and perfectly as he had come.

9

THAT NIGHT it did not go well with Kim Hartman, and in the morning Fox meditated at his window.

Today it was sunny, although the newspapers had promised rain.

"Mr. Fox, did you hear me buzz?" Miss Algur said.

Fox had heard nothing, but he heard Algur now. She was standing right next to him and snapped off her words the way she pounded her typewriter, as if she were blasting away on a huge old clacking vintage Remington.

"Sorry, Algur. What's up?"

"You have a *Mr.* Sneed on the line."

Miss Algur picked up Fox's telephone and handed it to him. She shut her eyes and floated out of the room like a disgusted parent.

"Sneed?"

"Hello, Foxy," Sneed said. "What's up?"

Talking to Sneed made Fox suddenly feel like a young associate again. Was the horrible feeling worth the possible information he might get from Sneed?

"Is there something wrong with your line?"

"That's just the sound of tape," Sneed answered, "Scotch magic transparent tape. Now that I'm a partner I'm so bored I do things like wrapping Scotch tape about my head."

In fact Sneed had done things like that when Fox had shared an office with him. That was one reason Sneed was now a partner in a big multinational go-go law firm, and not at Fox's stodgy Castle and Lovett.

"You don't think your colleagues will find that odd?" Fox asked.

"They won't notice it, Foxy," Sneed said. "You see, there's the antenna."

"The what?"

"The antenna I've taped to the back of my head. Made it with a coat hanger, Foxy. They don't see the tape because they're transfixed by the antenna. What's new?"

"Nothing," Fox said.

"That's what I thought," Sneed sneered. "It's been twelve years since we shared that office and you don't have anything new to report. We'll eat at the Kyoto, off Fifth, on Fifty-eighth. Next week I'm swinging a Japanese deal. I want to get in the mood."

"All right," Fox said. "That's fine."

"And, Foxy, let me give you a tip," Sneed said. "You're a partner now. You don't have to take the subway. You're a partner, and you can ride in a big yellow cab. Got it?"

Fox had gotten it all right, far too much. He hung up on Sneed.

Fox took the subway. As Gauder had once said, the subway is smellier, but faster. Then Fox walked across to Kyoto and found that Sneed, who had gotten them a private room, was now balding and looked like a Buddha in a vest: round, with a mysterious smile. Sneed did all the ordering, and Fox had no idea what he was getting.

"When did you pick that up?" Fox asked.

"The Japanese? I learned it in a Berlitz blitz course three weeks ago."

Fox told Sneed what he wanted to know, in plain old English.

"So you expect me to remember who the client

was that set up this little company that invested in one of Mr. Marsiglia's ventures, is that it?''

That was it. The waitress came with some seaweed. Sneed said something to her that made her blush.

"All this was when I was working with Brice Brothers," Sneed said. "All this was so long ago. Brice Brothers did not fit my image of myself. Neither did your shop."

"What image?"

"I don't know. I suppose I don't have one. I suppose that's part of my problem. First I worked in your place when we shared that disgusting office, and then I went with Brice and that didn't work either. I needed a fast place, Foxy. I was not going to make partner on the basis of hard work. I hate hard work. I needed a fast shop, with fast boys, where they would appreciate my special talents and forgive me my sins. Now, I fly in and out. Into Argentina for some deal. I stay locked in a hotel room in Buenos Aires for a week, but then it's done. Do you understand me? A week's stint is my logical working unit. I need to get revved up, blast in, blast out. In between I vegetate, grow cranky, act childish. I get bored easily."

"Do you remember anything about this deal?"

"Something, but I was not a big boy then. Brice Brothers did not trust their young flunkys. I recall assembling the corporation. It was, as you say, a vehicle to invest in a Marsiglia project. I remember the old wills too, Fox. I used to go into the file rooms and read them. What else was there to do? I used to sit down in a dusty corner, pull out some file, and see who was disinheriting whom. Jesus. See what I

39

remember? See what is stored in my mind? Yes, I remember that little investment vehicle. I remember the deal. I even glimpsed the client, who was, incidentally, in the deal for a lot less than three million two. I recall it all. A million one, I think. My mind is perfect, Fox. Look what I remember. But with a perfect mind comes boredom. What is there to figure out?''

''The client's name.''

''The client?''

''That's right.''

''Guess,'' Sneed said.

So Fox guessed. Sneed was vegetating, all right, and acting childish. But at least he didn't worry about the canons of ethics.

''Mrs. Belinda Meecham Sifford?''

''Wrong. Two more, Foxy.''

''Mr. Charles Sifford, Senior?''

''Tough luck. One guess left.''

''His son?''

''Ito kiwata nikito,'' Sneed said, with a huge smile.

''What the hell does that mean?''

''It means you've run out of guesses, but I'll tell you anyway.''

Actually, it meant ''you're a stuffed shirt.''

''Who was it?''

''Banning, a Mrs. Cora Banning.''

''Thanks for the information,'' Fox said. ''I appreciate it.''

''Anything for an old friend,'' Sneed said and smiled. ''After all, we did share an office in our youth. And, Fox, let me tell you one thing. I remember Mrs. Banning perfectly, because she had the butterfly. It was clearly there even though she tried to cover it with makeup.''

"Is this some kind of joke?"

"This is something even I wouldn't joke about. The butterfly is what they call the first sign of lupus. It is a spreading sort of rash, a mask over the face. Apparently it goes away as the disease gets worse. It always kills you in the end. Poor Mrs. Banning.''

Not exactly, Fox thought. She had a million one.

"How would you handle this?" Fox asked.

"Foxy, I would run down Mrs. Banning and see if she had any relationship to all those Siffords you seem to be interested in. But I would call Marsiglia first.''

"Why?"

"How long do you live with lupus? Mrs. Banning may very well be dead. But Marsiglia is alive, and very, very smart. Suppose he does have old Mrs. Sifford's money. Suppose he got it in an unorthodox way. Maybe he doesn't want any trouble to come back to haunt him. So you call him up, ask for your three million dollars, and he'll say, of course, Mr. Fox, your particular three million. Take it, it's yours, and don't bother me with details.''

"With questions," Fox said.

"You did say that Mr. Sifford disappeared from the face of the earth," Sneed said, smiling. "Details, Fox. Just details to the man who owns New York.''

10

SNEED AND FOX came out into the bright sunlight and walked around the corner to Fifth Avenue. The women here were beautiful all right, but with a faraway varnished look, almost as if they were museum pieces, under glass, and Fox imagined that there should be guards in black coats and hats behind them, telling you, "Tsk, tsk, do not touch the exhibition."

"How's Helen?" he said.

"Helen?" Sneed said. "I've got no idea. Divorce is in the offing."

There were hundreds of these varnished women on Fifth Avenue, so perfect looking it was hard for Fox to regard them as people. But they are, he reminded himself, and every damn one of them cares.

"Too bad," Fox said. "I'm sorry."

"Sorry? It's wonderful. I've surgically removed a thorn from my side. Being married to Helen was like having a small pebble in my sock. Just small enough that I went a long time without bothering to take my sock off and get rid of it. Look at all these women. Of course, you wouldn't care about women, would you, bachelor Fox?"

Sneed was wrong there. It was true that Fox was

into meditation, but he was also into Kim Hartman. And all these women made Fox feel like he wanted to misbehave. He wanted to pinch one of them. Or say something. There was a certain tension in the discrepancy between the psychological distance their glazed eyes projected and their physical closeness. You can't have the candy, they seemed to be saying, but we invite you to stick your nose right up to the glass and stare.

They passed Mikimoto, where there are nothing but beautiful perfect pearls in the window. Wonderful cultured pearls, New York pearls, each one of them exactly like the others, grown under the care and supervision of pearl scientists, New York pearls, Fifth Avenue pearls, because of their gloss and roundness and their being identical and somehow suspended between reality and illusion. Pearls, all right, but too perfect. In California, they like pearls that are not cultivated, but are discovered by accident, the kind that Japanese women still dive for wearing little goggles, each pearl different from the other, some of them looking like little shriveled oranges. In California, they wear pearls over T-shirts; in New York over bare skin that has been polished up like teak at Payot and decorated with silk around the edges.

Fox did not know all that, but he did know that Kim Hartman was a New York woman and that he was in love with her. Looking at the pearls, Fox developed a plan, involving the combining of two jobs into one, just the way Gauder had taught him. When he was dealing with Kim Hartman, Fox could actually, at times, be foxy.

"Pearls?" Sneed said, and squinted at Fox. "Pearls? Fox, are you losing your mind?"

11

ALGUR FUMED: Marsiglia's people had told her that if Fox wanted to talk to the boss, he would have to give his reasons personally. Not through a secretary. It took time, and he had to explain about Mrs. Sifford, but finally Fox was on hold, waiting for Marsiglia, and suddenly there was a roaring, thumping sound. A whacking, a pounding.

"What do you want?" It was hard to hear. What was Marsiglia doing? Was he at a construction site?

"This is Mr. Fox."

"I know that. What do you want?"

"To talk to you personally, privately."

"Why?"

"Mr. Marsiglia," Fox shouted into the phone, "I can't hear. The noise."

"The excavation? I'm so damn used to it, it doesn't bother me. All right, Mr. Fox." And then suddenly the whacking and thumping stopped. Had Marsiglia stopped a whole construction project with the wave of his hand?

"Satisfied? Now, what about Mrs. Sifford?"

"We have some problems with her estate. I would like to talk to you about them privately," Fox said.

"Talk."

"These are not matters to discuss over the phone," Fox said slowly, deliberately.

"Are you paranoid, Mr. Fox? What's the matter with you. You're worried about the phone? Where are your brains? It's my phone anyway."

His phone? Instinctively, Fox pulled the phone away from his ear and looked at it. "Quanta, Inc." was stamped on the receiver. Not Ma Bell, or anything Fox was familiar with. And then Fox remembered: the merger-making, go-go senior partner, Richard Lovett, had installed a new telecommunications system at the firm. His phone? Did Marsiglia own Quanta, Inc.?

"Talk, Mr. Fox. What's the matter with you?"

What was the matter? Marsiglia had hit on at least part of the problem: paranoia.

"Mr. Fox, I'm talking to you because of my old friend Mrs. Sifford," Marsiglia said. "What about her?"

"As you know," Fox finally said, "this firm represents her estate."

"So what?"

"We have an accounting problem."

"We?"

"Mr. Marsiglia," Fox blurted, thinking he had nothing to lose, "some money is missing from the estate. I was wondering if, possibly, Mrs. Sifford could have invested some funds with you. That is what I would like to discuss. Privately. Politely."

There was a roaring laugh that seemed to make Fox's telephone almost shake in his hands.

"I see, Mr. Fox. I understand. When I start out, they tell me that they won't give me money because I have no record. That I don't know anything about real estate. So what are they doing all the time? The bankers? The lawyers? They are losing the money of old women. I know you, Mr. Fox. I know your kind. All teak paneling and no brains."

"Mr. Marsiglia . . ."

"You lose some money, and now you think I am going to give it back to you. What do you think, Mr. Fox? That I'm going to open my closet and come out with a sack of gold and save your butt? You tell my people that I rented an apartment from Mrs. Sifford. So what? What are you going to do? Sue me? My lawyers sound just like you. They probably look just like you too. All of you seem to go to the same schools and have the same names. Castle and Lovett? Robert Fox? I tell you, to some people God gives classy names and bodies that look good in gray suits, and some people get funny names and all the brains."

"Listen," Fox demanded, angry now, realizing that Sneed was wrong. Marsiglia did not believe that it was in his best interest to talk things over quietly.

"To what? To you?"

"I don't like telephones, Mr. Marsiglia. I wanted to see if we could meet personally and talk quietly. There are a lot of other ways I could handle this."

"How much money did you lose, Mr. Fox? Tell me. I need to laugh."

"So you won't consider meeting with me."

"No. Sue me, Mr. Fox. Do anything you want.

Call the police. I don't talk to anybody. Old Mrs. Sifford never gave me any money. She should have, but she didn't."

And suddenly, the whacking and pounding started up again in the background, seeming louder than before. Why hadn't Marsiglia just hung up?

"Mr. Marsiglia," Fox shouted into the phone.

There was no answer, just the screeching sounds of construction. Slowly, delicately, Fox put his receiver down in its cradle. Then a sort of internal rumbling, pounding of his own took over, and he shouted: "Algur, get Jackson on the telephone in that warehouse. Tell him to work all night. I want a convection between a Mrs. Cora Banning and the Stifford estate."

12

HE WAS IN Kim Hartman's bed and wanted to make love. Kim could not make up her mind about it. Fox was a good lawyer, but not very good at coaxing.

"Whah do you know about lupus?" he asked. Kim's father had been a doctor.

She sat up, pulled the sheets around her, punched the rheostat, illuminating the carpeting that climbed up the walls, the smoked-glass mirrors, mounted on the walls, and the black Levolor blinds on the window.

"Who has it?"

"A Mrs. Banning."

"The wolf is after her. At the beginning, Fox, there's a sort of butterfly rash, that turns into markings like the black mask on some wolves' faces. Then the rash goes away, as the disease attacks your joints, your nerves, your spinal column. You creak, Fox. Finally, you die. That is lupus. Who is Mrs. Banning?"

"She was a sort of secretary-companion, to Mrs. Sifford."

"In that town house?"

"Yes."

"And where does she come from? How old is she? What's her maiden name?"

"I don't know. All Jackson has found out is that she's alive. Here in the city. We don't know where she came from. Does it matter?"

"Lupus is inherited, Fox. And ninety percent of the people who get it are female."

"That's crazy," Fox said sternly. "There is about one chance in a million that Mrs. Banning is your relative."

"My relatives are everywhere. It's the one chance in a million that kills you. Everything is connected. Everything comes back to get you."

"Absolutely nobody is going to 'get you,'" Fox said with conviction.

It didn't help. Kim Hartman stood up on the bed. In the mirrors, her tall body seemed to bounce around the room.

"Fox, a girl named Wanda was kicked out of school because she stole my pearls. That was twenty-five years ago. She'll come back. And following her will be all the dogs I've kicked, the slimy boys who thought they had some hold on me because they had a piece of my emotions for maybe twenty seconds, not to mention my body. I'm going to get pregnant, Fox, because I didn't use contraception fifteen years ago. It all comes back, everything, screaming back at you in the night."

She jumped off the bed, pulled on a yellow terry cloth robe and walked out of the room.

The long hall leading to the living room had tiny pinprick lights set in the ceiling. The carpeting was dark blue. Fox followed Kim's trail and found her sitting in the sunken, carpeted living room/conversation pit.

"I'm sorry I brought up Banning."

"Forget it. I'm past that now," Kim said quietly. "I'm thinking of myself, and why I wanted a mirror on the ceiling of my bedroom, a bed that floats on recessed lights, smoked-glass walls. What's wrong with me?"

He sat down next to her. "I love this place."

"I let some sleazy designer who wore tight pants and a loose jacket, who talked like Peter Lorre, and was named something like Gandolfo, I let him come here and rape me, not rape rape, just mind rape. He was thinking this old gal needs a place where she can get back into it, imagine herself making love. She needs action. I know what he was thinking, but why

49

did I want him to design the place that way? Why am I pathetic?''

Fox put his arm around Kim, pulled her in.

''You are definitely not pathetic.''

''I am a forty-year-old divorced mother fast proceeding toward menopause.''

''You don't look it. I love you. I want to marry you. I ask you every day.''

''I know it,'' she said. ''I love it.'' She leaned against him. ''And I won't do it.'' But she held his hand. ''This apartment is designed for lonely ladies, made to lure men. The mirrored bedroom is supposed to attract you the way your eyelashes attract me.''

Eyelashes? It sounded very strange to Fox: wasn't he supposed to have big muscles or something?

''Lashes?''

''My dear Fox, you have long dark lashes that make you look handsome and mysterious. And make me feel insecure because I'm the woman and I'm supposed to have even longer lashes. Do you understand?''

In a very dim way, Fox understood. Anyway, he felt better about his looks.

''And I'm also supposed to have enormous boobs, not these little things, and should want to mother you. I don't have the boobs, and I don't want responsibility either.''

''I look at advertisements,'' Fox told her softly. ''Large breasts are not in this year.''

''They used to be. Mothers stuffed Kleenex in their daughters' bras, girls were stupid and married too young. I need something, Fox, I'm scared. But the only answer I can come up with is redecorating this apartment, and I can't even figure that out. I don't know what I want to do, and the only part of the pathetic plan is that I know I want varnished lemon-colored wooden floors, soft as sand. Does that *mean* something?''

They went back to the bedroom, and set the lights very low. Kim spread herself out over Fox, her head lying in the corner of his shoulder, and whispered: "The wolf is after Mrs. Banning, Fox. The past is after me. Today, I thought the policeman knew I cheated the parking meter, and that the salesgirl at Saks knew it was the first store I ever shoplifted in. No life insurance salesmen called because they knew I was going to die. Fox, I've made so many mistakes that there's a whole army after me, a Mongol horde. I measure age in mistakes. I'm old. And the past is coming back, I can feel it, and the only answer I come up with is to redecorate."

"Marry me," Fox whispered. And put his arms around her back.

"Marry me, marry me," she whispered back. "Do you ask me because you know it hits me in the stomach in a physical way, makes me want to make love?"

In fact, they were already doing it.

13

THE BLAGDEN BUILDING was a beautiful building that seemed to float on the fountains that Marsiglia had put in. The columns that held the building were very thin and elegant, and somehow Marsiglia had made the huge height of the building not overpowering. It had something to do with the recessed glass, Fox thought, curving in, not bulging out, so that the building seemed porous. It was, he decided, the image of New York, where there are liveried doormen and the women always get out of long black cars, dressed in mink and laughing.

The Blagden Building was also a "convection" Jackson had noted, connecting Mrs. Banning and Marsiglia.

The hallway of Mrs. Banning's apartment had the same grace and sense of solid money. It also had a pretty young man with black pants and a white coat and maybe the finest set of white teeth that Fox had ever seen.

"I have an appointment with Mrs. Banning," Fox said.

The boy with the white teeth blocked the hall as if he was unsure about that. He had a proprietary sense about this graceful apartment which reminded Fox of a goalkeeper on a soccer field when the other team has a free kick. The white coat said servant, but the big forced smile that showed the pretty teeth said thug.

"You don't seem to understand," Fox suggested. "I spoke with her yesterday."

"So?"

The big smile looked like something you would have to practice in the mirror to get straight, Fox thought. Where does he use it? In bars?

"Please let me in," Fox said. "Please don't argue with me. I have an appointment."

"Up yours," the smiler said.

Generally, Fox was very considerate. But he could also be a little dangerous. He was a big, strong man. Now Fox looked at the pretty boy with the rage of a wounded eleven-foot-tall Alaskan grizzly, confronting a four-foot hunter who has run out of bullets.

"Out of my way," Fox roared. "Go to the wall. Stand against it as if you were a quiet rubber tree plant, or I will take your little white coat and turn it around and tie the arms behind you. I think you will look very good in a strait jacket."

He had made his point at last, and the boy went running down the long hall.

Fox found a large, green, flower-filled room that had a spectacular view of the city. There was no one in it, but he could hear something coming. First there was a sliding sound, and then a thwack, then the sliding, then another thwack.

There was too much to take in at one time as Mrs. Banning made her entrance. The first thing Fox caught was the walker: it was made out of aluminum, about four feet tall, like a small steel podium or the frame of a lecture stand. It must have been very light, because Mrs. Banning threw it ahead of her, it thwacked on the floor, and then she took a step forward, using the walker as a crutch. She threw it with such power that Fox thought, suddenly, it is not a walker, it's a warrior's shield. Why does she look as if she's attacking? Fox wondered. Mrs. Banning looked only about fifty years old, but her disease made her move like an arthritic old invalid, her long neck extended forward like a racehorse, her powerful, pointed jiggling chin leading the way. It was such a sight that Fox almost didn't notice that the smiler was behind her. Mrs. Banning got over to a large couch, kicked her walker away, and free-fell into what looked to Fox like a pillow filled with twenty inches of pure down.

"Thank you for seeing me," Fox said.

The boy took a position behind the couch and smiled at Fox, a taunting smile that seemed to say, Now it's your turn.

"For what?" Mrs. Banning snapped. "If I don't see you now, I'll have to see you later. I just want to see you once. What is it? Why are you hounding me?"

Hounding? Fox thought. How do I handle this? What would Gauder have done?

"Mrs. Banning," Fox said slowly, "I am very sorry to have disturbed you. I'll try to be brief."

"Good," she said.

"We have a continuing problem with the estate of Mrs. Belinda Meecham Sifford."

"You are not being brief. Continuing problem? Please don't use those words. Say what you want. What is it? What do I have to do with it?"

"First, Mrs. Banning," Fox said slowly, "you worked for Mrs. Sifford, and presumably know something about her affairs."

"Worked for her?" Mrs. Banning snapped. With that, she flicked out her foot, in a quick movement that surprised Fox, caught the walker, picked it up and stamped it down hard on the floor. "I was her paid flunky," she snorted.

"I don't understand," Fox said. "I thought you were an intimate companion."

"Of course I was intimate with her. Who else was? I was so intimate with her that I would be ordered to sit and listen to her for months on end. We went on cruises together, Mr. Fox. I was seasick most of the time, locked in a goddamned cabin listening to an old bitch bark. And Mrs. Sifford barked all the time, Mr. Fox. She barked about her mother and her father and her son and the world situation, and you can bet your life that she knew exactly what was best for all of them. She knew what was best for her servants, the president, Congress, and everyone who lives in this city. She knew exactly what was best for me as well, and she told me what to wear, when to smile, and what to say, usually in front of other

55

people. Now *I* have barked, Mr. Fox. You do the same."

Her monologue seemed to have relieved her a little; she leaned back in the big soft sofa.

"Did she ever confide in you about her business dealings?" Fox asked, debating when to bring up the investment with Marsiglia.

"What business dealings? What business did she have but to clip her coupons at the New York Trust Company? What in God's name are you talking about? She had a big fat checkbook and a big fat pen, and when she wanted a big fat something, she put the two of them together. Do you think she knew anything about stocks? When she bought those, it was mad money. I suppose I should offer you tea. Do you want any?"

"No thank you," Fox said.

"Too bad," Mrs. Banning said. "I pay for Randolph. I might as well get some use out of him." The fat smile disappeared from Randolph's face. "Now tell me exactly what you want to know, Mr. Fox."

Fox decided it was time. Mrs. Banning had offered him tea. He didn't think she would get more relaxed than that. Gauder would have done it now, he thought.

"Mrs. Banning, thirteen years ago, the Meecham Building was mortgaged by Mrs. Sifford for three million two hundred thousand dollars. That money has disappeared."

"I see," Mrs. Banning said. And now she leaned forward, her hand on the walker, supporting her body. "I see that you do not understand Mrs.

Sifford. And therefore, you are making stupid, blundering insinuations. Try to listen to me, Mr. Fox. I do not have time for mistakes. Mrs. Sifford believed in God, and in the inevitability of God's law. She was rich. Why? God had rewarded her because she was perfect. I was poor. My husband had left me because I was a sinner. For Mrs. Sifford, misfortune only happened to sinners. And because I was one, I was punished. A strange, old-fashioned mind, Mr. Fox. She believed in revenge, punishment, and that everything was part of God's secret plan. That was Mrs. Sifford. She would not have wanted to upset God's obvious desire to humiliate me by giving me any of her money. And I'm sure the old bitch believed that the tirades and tongue lashings she gave me, her husband, and her son, I'm sure she thought she was only helping God carry out some devious, inevitable plan to punish us, and therefore save our souls."

"But she hired you."

"Not out of pity, Mr. Fox. She liked to have sinners around to remind herself how perfect she was. She was the kind who got her kicks out of watching sinners suffer. I am tired, Mr. Fox, and sick. But at least I have been direct with you. Try and be the same with me."

"Mrs. Banning, thirteen years ago, you invested at least one million dollars with Mr. Marsiglia, in a real estate syndicate that built this apartment house. And you were poor. Where did you get a million dollars?"

"You are stupid," Mrs. Banning burst out. "And misinformed. I never got any money from

Mrs. Sifford. I never got a damn thing. Am I a liar?''

She looked up at Randolph, as if she was giving him some sort of signal. Gauder had trained Fox in many ways, but there were situations that even Gauder had not encountered. Fox went on anyway.

"Perhaps Mrs. Sifford's advisors didn't want her to invest with Marsiglia. Perhaps she didn't want to hurt their feelings. So she asked you to invest for her."

"She did not."

"Or perhaps she gave you the money as a gift, for services rendered."

The aluminum walker was rattling now, even though Mrs. Banning had both hands on it.

"We can talk about this some other time," Fox suggested.

"We will never talk again," Mrs. Banning hissed. "I shall straighten out your stupidity and then you will never hound me again."

"All right," Fox said.

"I can see that you think me a liar and a fool." She rattled her walker. "You want to take away my money. I can see that clearly, too."

"I don't want to do anything to you," Fox said quickly.

"You're not going to, Mr. Fox. I am going to make you understand. I have told you I have no idea what happened to her money. I suppose it went with her husband. Blood money to get him out of her life. She did not like divorce. She did not tolerate scandal. After all, she was perfect."

"She hated her husband?" Fox said.

"Yes. Of course. Aren't you listening? Jesus God. How do I make you understand? Do I have to tell you everything? Why would you hate your wife, Mr. Fox?"

"I don't have one."

"I knew you had problems. I can see clearly that you are stupid. You would hate your wife if you caught her with another man. Now do you understand, Mr. Fox? I was poor and my husband had left me. Therefore, to Mrs. Sifford, I had to be a whore. That was inevitable. To her warped, vile mind. Why else would a husband leave? My mind works somewhat differently, Mr. Fox. If I'm treated as a whore, I'll act like one. Do you understand now, Mr. Fox? I am the last person in the world to whom Mrs. Sifford would have given money. And if I had taken any from her, she would have made sure to get it back. She would have hounded me, Mr. Fox, the way you are hounding me now, even into hell."

Fox looked intently at Mrs. Banning. There was something sensual about her, despite the disease and her savage temperament. A sort of animal, instinctual beauty lay centered in her round arms, large body, black hair. The disease had taken its toll, but Fox could still imagine Mrs. Banning in bed, greedily and pleasurably devouring a man.

"I understand," he said. He did: thirteen years ago, Mrs. Banning could walk. And make love. Mrs. Sifford had caught Mrs. Banning in bed with her husband.

"Mrs. Sifford never gave me anything except hell," Mrs. Banning said, and now there was real emotion in her voice. "She threw me out, and left me desperate. She would not have given me three million dollars. She wouldn't have given me one. I got together a million in every way I could, from my friends. I am not a nice person, Mr. Fox. I forced some of them to loan me money. I knew Marsiglia was smart, unlike you, and he was desperate too, running out of money to finish this apartment house. I gave the money to Marsiglia, and knew that if it didn't work, I would kill myself. I wanted to live in a certain style, in the time I had left."

"Do you have any idea where Mr. Sifford is?" Fox asked.

"Don't hound me, Mr. Fox. I haven't seen or heard from the bastard these past thirteen years. Find your own way out."

"But you were involved with him," Fox said. "He's never communicated?"

The walker shook violently. "Understand me, Mr. Fox. I am dying. So I am direct and truthful with you. Why not? There isn't time for anything else. Don't hound me."

"Did Mr. Sifford tell you where he was going? Did he ever speak about places he'd like to go?"

"I said don't hound me. If I wanted to, Mr. Fox, I could have Randolph shoot you here and now. Only three of us are present. What jury is going to convict a dying woman? Do you want to die, Mr. Fox?"

The big fat smile was back on Randolph's face.

Fox realized that this was definitely not something Gauder had prepared him for. He stood up.

"Thank you so very much for talking to me," he said, heading for the door, moving like a real fox that the hounds were chasing.

PART TWO

The Highwayman

14

THEY CAME TO AN intersection, on their way to the West Side Highway. Going the opposite direction was a black van, with all the gadgets: smoked-glass heart-shaped windows, mag wheels, and an exhaust stytem designed to compete with the blasting hi-fi.

"See what's on the bumper?" Kim Hartman said.

Fox hadn't seen—he was trying to drive.

" 'To hell with disco, to hell with soul, us white boys like rock and roll,' " Kim quoted. "You know what that means?"

"No," Fox said.

The hardest part of the trip was getting out of the city. He didn't want an accident to ruin all his plans.

"It means race war," Kim Hartman said.

"Listen, Kim," Fox said, "let me drive for a while."

The light had changed and the charging van almost

sideswiped him. It *was* full of white boys. One of them gave Fox the finger.

"This city is falling apart," Kim said.

"Look, Kim," Fox said, "it's not all that bad. The man I'm going to see, Charles Sifford, Junior, scion of one of New York's oldest families, has, coincidentally, the same name as one of the most famous golfers in the United States. A millionaire black golfer. Things do change."

"Nothing changes," Kim Hartman said. "The only hopeful sign is that the silly van is going into the city and we're going away."

They made it to the West Side Highway, the wall of apartments on the right and the river on the left.

"You know Fluffy?" Kim said. "She packs a rod. She's a paranoid schizo, and a graduate of Radcliffe. I think I was wrong to hire her."

Kim Hartman was talking about a young college graduate she'd hired to help her in the art appraisal business. Miss Fluffy Ravenel from Charleston, South Carolina. Fluffy was working with Kim in the Sifford town house.

"I ask for a Kleenex, and of course, Fluffy wants to please me, so she begins going through her purse. The Kleenex, it appears, is right at the bottom of it, and innocently all her little goodies get laid out on my desk. I see her pills, her notebook, address book, glasses case, makeup, and then she pulls out this gun and sort of tosses it on top of all the rest of the junk. Then Fluffy gives me a Kleenex. I thought it was some kind of cigarette lighter. But, it's a real honest-to-God, full-of-bullets little pistol. You see what I mean?"

"Why does she have it?" Fox said.

They went over a bridge, into the Bronx, heading for the foul concrete of the near suburbs—where the enclosed shopping malls are like endless walls of empty concrete billboard, all surrounded by dead cars.

"Her daddy said it was good for her. New York is such a mean place. Daddy expects her to plug some rapist. I don't know why she has to have it. Southern girls. Southern men."

Kim Hartman was a Southern girl too. Her family had come from Richmond, Virginia. She had gone to dances there, growing up. All this, she had told Fox many times, had been an intensely painful experience, and Kim had paid a psychiatrist many thousands of dollars in order to live the painful experience all over again.

"I'm looking at this gun, lying on my desk. Yes, it actually does have a pearl handle. It's only about three inches long. And I'm scared out of my wits just looking at the thing. And all the time, Miss Fluffy Ravenel is going on with this inane conversation, telling me what an interesting day she had yesterday, and how happy she is working for me. All the time there is a gun on my desk. What do I do?"

"Fire her," Fox said.

"You're right," Kim said, "I'll fire her. That's all you can say? Fire her? Aren't you interested?"

Fox didn't want to think about guns. "Just tell her she can't bring the gun to the office," he said.

They had finally gotten past Yonkers and White Plains. It didn't take much time. The road seemed designed to make the experience as short as possible. It was about ten lanes wide, a sort of apology for the disgusting character of the place. The big road seemed to say: what you're going to experience is horrible all right, but we'll get you through it fast. And that was the way all those suburban drivers—first in the big station wagons and then the little Omnis—took the road, Fox thought. All of them driving like Omnizombies, not using their directional signals, blasting down the highway toward another of their enclosed malls.

At least in the city, Fox thought, you walk between the buildings—here it's all cars, highway, or the inside of a mall, and you don't see a thing. Plus, there are no eccentrics, he thought, and no winos. What wino could exist here? This place has no doorways, no back alleys, no benches.

"Fluffy Ravenel is taking her gun out on dates," Kim Hartman said. "We never did that. We should have, but we didn't. There are a lot of boys I would have liked to shoot. It was just that nobody told me I could. My daddy never said: 'Here, take this along. If Allen doesn't behave himself, plug him.' You know what I mean? I had to fight tooth and nail. In big white dresses with bows, I had to kick drunk boys in tuxedos in the balls . . . Well, you know, Fox. I could have made a lot of boys shape up a lot more easily with a rod."

"Why do you call Fluffy's gun a rod?"

"Fox, I don't call it that, she calls it that. I don't know. I don't understand Fluffy at all. What's happened to this generation?"

Fox had no idea, so he didn't answer.

Now the highway went down to two lanes and they were in the country. The river came into view again:

huge. And the steep mountains seemed to float down into it. There were a lot of twists and folds in both the river and the mountains.

"This section always reminds me of Scotland," Fox said.

"Of course it reminds you of Scotland," Kim said. "It's reminded a lot of other people of Scotland, too. That is why it is called the Hudson River Highlands."

In both places, Fox thought, Scotland and the Hudson Highlands, there was something that cast a vaguely suspicious aura. You could get lost in these twisting gullies lined with trees, or come upon some-one unexpectedly. Now and then huge houses appeared suddenly on the tops of hills. The houses, built by the railroad barons at the turn of the century, looked harsh. That was a part of the sinister nature of the region.

"I missed everything," Kim Hartman said. "No coed dorms, no easy sex, no guns under the pillow. I was ruined in my childhood. There was a huge tidal wave riding along behind me. There were hippies, yippies, revolution, and San Francisco to come. Here I was, a couple of years too early, still thinking that it was acceptable behavior to always have the boy try to rape you after a dance and never complain, that it was perfectly normal after that kind of thing for him to come into the house and converse pleasantly with my parents. Maybe Fluffy's right. Let her keep the gun. I don't care, as long as she doesn't point it at me. I like the idea that her parents are protective. Mine never were.

"My mother thought my breasts weren't large

enough. Is that the sign of an intelligent mother? To tell your daughter to stuff Kleenex in her bra at her coming-out party? My mother had been the belle of the ball. Huge bazoomas. She just wanted the same thing for me. She didn't understand. The gentlemen were long gone, replaced by thugs. There was a sea change under way. Just behind me was a mob of crazies heading to San Francisco. With me, riding my wave, spearheading my generation, it was just a bunch of dumb thugs disguised in tuxes.''

They were off the highway now, on the small roads that twisted in the mountains next to the river. Here the gas stations seemed to leap at you when you rounded a bend, and had individual names: like ''Red's'' or ''Bill's.'' Rusted cars sat next to the stations, and each had a junk heap, and Red or Bill still fixed cars out of the junk heap, and Red or Bill looked suspicious, and actually eyed each driver directly with a leery eye.

''Fox, can I try to explain something to you?''

''Anything at all,'' Fox said.

''My mother always told me I looked just like my dear aunt Leda. Now dear Aunt Leda was a drunk, and had a mint julep for breakfast, Fox. It took me ten years to figure out that my mother was referring to dear Aunt Leda's childhood. When they had both been children, Leda looked a lot different. She was actually pretty. But here I was, seventeen, thinking I looked like an old hag. I hadn't seen Leda in the flower of her youth.

''That's how we get messed up. The generations don't mesh. Do you understand what I'm trying to say.''

"Yes," Fox said, and added: "You sure are talking a lot."

She immediately stopped talking. Fox had meant: I love it that you're talking to me, that you can talk to me. I love you. But too many conversations with too many lawyers had numbed his brain and he didn't get his point across with Kim Hartman.

They came to the sign that said ARDEONUIG HOTEL and turned into a well-kept secluded private drive. At the end of it was a lovely, small, white two-story building that stood beside a stream. A bronze plaque over the door said ARDEONUIG HOTEL in letters so small you had to squint to read them. Beside HOTEL was the date, 1868, that the place had been built. In a certain circle in New York this was a very famous place.

"Now I see the full extent of your plan," Kim Hartman said. "And I approve."

15

THEY HAD made love. In a room that had newly sanded lemon-colored wooden floors, laid down over a hundred years before and soft as sand. It had white curtains and a white bed, and they had drunk a bottle of white wine from room service.

This hotel offered only room service, so that the

guests did not embarrass each other by meeting in a dining room. No one had been embarrassed here in over one hundred years. To Fox, all of it had been wonderful, and he was thinking that early the next morning, he would sneak out before his meeting with Charles Sifford, Jr., and try for trout.

That was the excuse for the hotel, and the reason men had given for over one hundred years for visiting it. Time for trout fishing, they told their wives.

And indeed, there was fine trout fishing, but that was not, of course, why they had gone to the hotel. Fox felt wonderful and wondered if maybe Mr. Sifford, Sr., had ever gone trout fishing here with Mrs. Banning. He was feeling fine, but Kim Hartman, lying next to him in the bed, had a sort of puzzled, even annoyed look on her face.

"What?" Fox said.

"You asked me if I wanted to make love."

"Yes. And you did," Fox said.

"You're so polite," she said. "You ask if I'll marry you. You ask if you can make love with me. You know what I mean?"

"I have no idea what you mean."

"Consider the people who've been here. You don't exactly sweep me off my feet. Think of Stanford White and that girl. Where did Grover Cleveland do it with his mistress? Think of John Kennedy. Was he ever here? I don't know. Probably. And you *ask* if we can make love. You know what I mean?"

"Not exactly," Fox said. Cautiously.

"What do I expect," Kim Hartman said, looking

at the ceiling. "You didn't exactly jump me. But why should you? What have you got? You've got a forty-year-old mother."

"One who looks like she had her kid at thirteen and spent the rest of her life exercising," Fox said, thinking that, in fact, that was exactly how Kim Hartman did look. She looked wonderful. What is forty? Fox wondered. What's going on in her mind? Menopause? Jesus, that would mean we couldn't have children together. Well, he thought, we would already have one. Anyway, it's not menopause, he thought, because she's using an IUD, and what's wrong with me that my mind works this way? Why can't I let my mind float?

"What happened? Was my mind permanently injured growing up when boys tried to rape me? What do I expect?" She stopped talking to the ceiling, turned to Fox, and snuggled in next to him. "Listen," she said, "forgive me. Sometimes I think I'm not going to recognize a good man when I see one, and it's going to cost me plenty."

"Have I got this straight?" he asked. "You think I'm a dolt?"

"Dolt?" she said. "What a word."

"Boring?"

"You're not boring. You're sweet."

"Not given to impulsive, romantic gestures? Not given to wanting to molest you in phone booths?"

Fox got out of bed. And pretended to storm around the room. Pretended that he was packing his bag. He wasn't. He was searching through it.

"Listen," Kim Hartman said, sitting up. "Don't leave!"

Fox shook his head, his back to her.

"Look," she said. "For God's sake."

He turned around, the box in his hand, and threw her the pearls from Mikimoto. Then he got back in bed.

"Is this a ring?" Now *she* sounded suspicious. "I won't take a ring."

"Here? No."

"Good." She opened the box carefully, as if it might be booby-trapped.

They were beautiful pearls. Fox got excited looking at them. She was the one who was supposed to get excited, of course, but they looked so perfect and otherworldly Fox could not believe that he, himself, had actually gone out and purchased them. First she held them gently. Then she rubbed them all together. Then she let them dangle from one end, holding them to the light. Then she put them back in the box. Then she opened the box again, put them on, got out of bed, and went to look in the mirror. She was naked except for the pearls. But somehow they were enough to make her look dressed. She turned around and faced Fox.

"Yes," she said.

"Yes what?"

"Just yes," Kim Hartman said. "Giving me pearls, here and now, is exactly what I want. Forget being raped and whatever else I said. This is exactly the right blend of illicit sex, ruthlessness, power, wealth, whoredom, surprise, and everything else everyone else seems to be enjoying. Thanks.'' She came over to the bed. "Besides," she added.

"Besides what?'' Fox said.

"Besides, the old Southern saying goes that once you get their pearls off, Southern girls love to fuck.''

16

FLUFFY RAVENEL, twenty-two and from South Carolina, packs a rod, Fox thought. Well, I have a "rod" of my own.

It was eight and a half feet of bamboo, made by the Leonard Rod Company, came in three sections, and weighed just a couple of ounces. Fox assembled it by his car, put on his waders and vest, and headed toward the stream. It was about five-thirty, and a white mist spread out through the trees. In the places where there was grapevine, the white mist was like the froth on the top of big green waves.

Fox did not understand grapevine at all. Where it grew, it destroyed the trees, and then eventually itself. It climbed steadily up the tree trunks in green sheets of thick leaves and grapes, jumped from branch to branch, from tree to tree, until finally, it had spread a blanket over a section of forest. Of course, then, the trees did not get sunlight and they eventually rotted and fell; the blanket of grapevine fell with the trees, collapsing on top of itself, and dying too on the forest floor. But grapevine only grew in certain sections. Some trees, whole areas of trees, seemed immune to it, as if protected by some forest god. You could whack at grapevine, cutting it down, trying to find the taproots, but where it did grow, no matter how much you attacked it or how long, you could not get rid of it. It eventually had to kill itself. A New York plant, Fox thought.

This was a New York forest, with the trees close together, but little underbrush, the earth soft and damp, and the land spotted with large boulders, jagged rock formations, and gulleys. Fox heard the stream before he saw it. It was small: maybe thirty feet across. It twisted around in the forest. Fox stepped into it at a bend. The water here was only about four inches deep, and rushing over many colored pebbles. Maybe twenty yards downstream, the little stream took a quick turn, running out of sight. Where it turned, a big boulder stuck up out of the water. There was green moss on it, at the water line. The white morning mist seemed to flow with the little stream, perhaps drawn along by the coldness of the water. The stream went across Fox's feet, and the white mist softly swirled past him.

Fox let his line float downstream toward the boulder, letting the curves and twists built into the line's memory from its long storage on the reel get washed clean in the flow of the water. The line slithered away from Fox, down toward the boulder, and the bend in the stream. It snaked in rich curves like a picture being drawn by an artist with a delicate hand, the line's curves following the strongest pull in the stream.

When the line was almost to the boulder, Fox stopped the spinning of the reel by pressing his palm on the spool. The curving picture erased itself, and the line went straight in the water, pulled taut by its own weight. Fox let the line lie that way for a while as he studied the stream. Then, holding the rod with his right hand, he hauled the line back in, not using the reel, but making the line into a coil held in his left hand. When the line was about fifteen feet from Fox, he pulled up on the rod. The line rose out of the water in an arch, slowly sliding through the mist, back over Fox's head. He barely moved the rod forward, letting out coils with his left hand, and the line flicked forward in a slow motion dance that cut the mist. Each time barely moving the arm that held the rod, Fox threw the line forward and backward, each time letting out more line until the small fly, not larger than the fingernail of his smallest finger, poised for a fraction of a second over the boulder.

He let it drop. The fly on the other side of the boulder, away from Fox, the line itself lying on top of the boulder, and then the fish hit. It had hit on the first cast, and taken the hook tight, and it jumped up on the other side of the boulder, turning in the air, and then went down again, fighting to go downstream around the bend. When the fish ran, Fox gave it line, and when the pull was steady, he took in line, moving downstream toward the boulder, and also trying to work the fish around the side of the boulder, move him away from it, so that the thin leader would not cut on the hard granite. Finally, the fish came out into the open, into the stream on Fox's side of the boulder, jumping, twisting, trying to dart back then moving forward again. Fox took in the line, until finally the rod was almost bent double. The fish was right at Fox's feet and still moving, darting. Fox held the line tight with his right hand, which held the rod too, reached down with his left, and pinned the fish, holding it facing the flow of the current. He held his rod now between his arm and his body and both hands were on the fish as he used the tweezers from his vest to carefully extract the barbless hook. Even when the hook was out, he held the fish, until he could feel it now struggling again, its breath back, and then he let it go. He could not see it go. It moved too quickly. One cast. He waded out of the stream and went back to the car in his waders, their padded bottoms sponge-full of water. Well, well, he thought, proud of himself, for once. Seven hundred dollars' worth of equipment, big waders that make me look like the clown with the big pants, and then one cast. It's worth it.

17

KIM HARTMAN did not go with Fox to visit Charles Sifford, Jr., and Mrs. Sifford. Why should she go? She could stay in the room, order what she wanted, and then walk in the woods. Fox left her, drove for ten minutes along the small road, turned in past two large stone gateposts that had no name on them, drove up a long drive that climbed one of those Hudson River hills, and suddenly entered a gravel turnaround that encircled a large flat expanse of green grass. Behind that was a large stone one-story house.

It was the same house: the huge old mansion in the painting by Frederick Church. The painting worth seven fifty that hung in the Sifford town house. But there was a difference: the upper three floors had been removed.

It's a good job, Fox thought. The new roof was long and wide, with deep overhangs, so that the massive stone walls that had supported the upper floors still seemed justified. The front door was open. Fox rang the bell and peered inside. Nothing happened for a long time. Then a short, solidly built plain woman came around the bend of the big hall. Her red sneakers made a suction sound on the stone floor. The woman was Mrs. Charles Sifford, Jr., and she had an open face, a plain cotton dress, and a no-nonsense manner as she took Fox through the living room into a glassed-in porch where her husband, Charles Sifford, Jr., sat in a lounge chair, reading a newspaper.

"Junior," Mrs. Sifford said, "Mr. Fox is here."

"Hello, Mr. Sifford," Fox said. "Nice to see you again."

Junior Sifford got right up and shook Fox's hand vigorously. His wife asked if Fox wanted some tea or juice, and then they got down to work, signing the papers.

Fox had expected some sort of inquiry about the general condition of the estate. Some questions on the judgments he had made. Nothing like that happened. He gave them papers, and Mr. Sifford signed them. He did so pleasantly and wholeheartedly, and for the first time since Fox had been involved with the Sifford matter, he felt that he had come across some people who were not dangerous, lying, conniving, or mean.

"Is that it?" Junior said. He rubbed his hands together, as if he was all ready to sign everything all over again, and smiled at Fox.

"Almost," Fox said. "There's a matter I want to discuss with you."

"All right. Fine."

"Thirteen years ago, your mother took some three million dollars and did something with it, Mr. Sifford," Fox said. "Actually, the money just disappeared thirteen years ago."

"Well, I see," Mr. Sifford said, looking expectantly at Fox. His plain wife was sitting next to him. Apparently, Mr. Sifford didn't see. When Fox didn't say anything, Junior looked at his wife for guidance.

"Well, there's plenty of money, Junior," Mrs. Sifford said to her husband. He nodded thoughtfully. The woman gave him a reassuring smile, that seemed to put Mr. Sifford at complete ease despite the fact that he'd just been told of the loss of three million of his money, or of what would eventually be his money when everything was finished. This man is the grandson of the Meecham that blasted a whole railroad through the granite of these mountains, Fox thought, the heir to a fortune. And he doesn't understand a thing, or doesn't want to understand. Interesting.

"Well?" Junior said.

"Can I ask you a few questions?" Somehow Fox felt he had to ask if he *could* ask. Why did he feel that?

"All right. Shoot."

"Thirteen years ago, to get this money, your mother signed a mortgage. You cosigned the mortgage, Mr. Sifford. Do you remember that?"

"No," he said, "I don't remember, but I'm sure I did sign."

"You don't remember the transaction?"

"No," he said, "I don't." He looked again at his wife. She looked straight at Fox, as if she were a judge who at any moment might bang down the gavel and rule a question out of order.

"I wonder if you remember any dealings with Marsiglia?" Fox said.

Suddenly, Mr. Sifford's eyes blinked. He smiled, came alive.

"Do I remember some dealings with Marsiglia?" he boomed. "Of course I remember dealings with him. I've been dealing with him all my life. Why didn't you say so? Sure."

Now his wife held on to his hand.

"Well, what?" Mr. Sifford said. "You want to talk to him? Right now, Marsiglia and I are working on a project. In the south field. You ought to see it. We've cleared the whole thing. All the boulders are out. Next we're going to put in the trees. You know what kind? Elm trees. All the elms are going with the disease, but we're putting them back. What do you think?"

"Marsiglia?" Fox said, confused.

"Yes," Mr. Sifford said. "Who else?"

"He's talking about Marsiglia's son, the builder," Mrs. Sifford said to her husband. She was still holding his hand.

"His son?"

"In New York."

"I know him, of course," Mr. Sifford said slowly. "But never had any dealings with him, Mr. Fox. I see him. He comes up here regularly to see his father."

"His father works for you?"

Mr. Sifford nodded thoughtfully.

"I don't think you'd say he works for me," he said finally. He looked at his wife. "Would you?" he said to her. She shook her head. He turned back to Fox. "I'd say we sort of work together now, if you understand. He worked for my grandfather and for my mother, you know—he was born here—but we've sort of changed things, as you see. He's got his own house and his own money. I wouldn't say he works for me. I'd say we work together. He's very old. How old is he?" Again, turning to his wife.

"Eighty-three," she said.

"Eighty-three," Mr. Sifford said. "He's eighty-three, you see. This used to be an awful big place, Mr. Fox. I mean, there were people who were born here. You know all about these old places."

"Yes," Fox said.

"I'll tell you what I remember exactly," Mr. Sifford said. "I remember exactly how this place was when I was ten or so, and we would ride up from New York in the special train for the weekend. You know how long it took us to get here? Forty minutes. No stops—my grandfather made them really move that train. He used to love to get up here for the weekend. I remember all of that. But you can't keep going that way, can you?''

"No,'' his wife said.

"First of all, it isn't fair for the country. Do you read me, Mr. Fox? I don't think all of that was right. I've thought it all through and I don't think that we did things in the proper way. You get a train now for New York City, and I hear it takes you hours to get in. But I still don't think it was right that one person should have all the money. Do you understand me? That is what I honestly believe. We both do.''

"Now, thirteen years ago,'' Fox began.

"I don't know, Mr. Fox,'' Junior Sifford said suddenly. "I don't know about thirteen years ago. I don't know what I signed. I don't want to talk about thirteen years ago. You know I'm tired as hell.'' He looked at his wife.

"Of course you are,'' she said, and stood up. His wife had him by the arm. He reached out and took Fox's hand. Then he went off by himself down the hall, shaking his head.

18

Fox WAS left alone with Mrs. Sifford. The glassed-in porch was a pretty room, with light, airy furniture and a shaggy rug over the stone floor. But even that could not completely hide the feeling Fox got from the house. This place had been a mansion, and yes, it was something different now, something definitely more pleasant perhaps, but there was still the lingering effect of the big thick walls, the high ceilings, the stone floor. The house had been built to intimidate—then taken apart in an attempt to let ordinary people gain dominance over it. Not baronial magnates with private trains who blasted up for the weekend on their railroads. The woman must have been responsible for the rebuilding, Fox realized. She'd taken on the wealth and the building, and had fought it to a draw.

"I'm sorry if I upset Mr. Sifford," Fox said.

"What can you do?" she said. "You have a problem. But you'll resolve it to everyone's satisfaction, won't you."

Won't you. The way she said it—it was not a plea for help, but an implicit instruction. You will. That was what she had said. Again the professional tone in her voice set off vague rumblings of remembrance in the backwaters of Fox's mind.

"Thirteen years ago, this money disappeared," Fox said. "And Mr. Sifford's father ran away from his family. Obviously, it was a trying time, and I can understand his reluctance to recall it. The domestic upheaval must have been very painful."

The woman sat down across from Fox.

"My husband had gone about drinking away his mind a good while before those events," she said crisply. "His mother was an interesting woman."

"What sort of a woman?"

"I don't know what to say, or how it would help, Mr. Fox. I suppose she was a good woman, but no good for her son. You must realize the other side of the coin. Mrs. Sifford's father, old Baron Meecham, who built this place—well, you must know about him. But Mrs. Sifford's mother, Mrs. Meecham, was deeply struck by religion in a way particular to these Highlands. How can I explain it to you?

"Mr. Fox, here they use divining rods to find the spot to put in a well. Perfectly normal men thrash about in the bushes, following the pull of little twigs they are holding in their hands. And the peculiar thing is, after living here thirteen years, I am beginning to believe in it myself. Old Mrs. Meecham was just an ordinary young woman whose family had lived here for generations. She was not rich. Suddenly, she was the richest woman in the world. Her world at least. She had married the Baron. And she thought she didn't deserve it. To Mrs. Meecham, you only deserved that much money if you were Jesus Christ. Does any of this make any sense to you, Mr. Fox?"

"Yes," Fox said.

"The Meechams, the Siffords. They are all extremely peculiar people. But then I suppose anyone who builds a railroad is peculiar."

Fox thought of the young Marsiglia, building New York City. What were his eccentricities?

"How did all this affect Mrs. Sifford?" he asked, and because he was himself a little confused by all this genealogy, added, "I mean your husband's mother."

"In several interesting ways. I will give you an example. On Christmas the toys were all laid out; they were opened and examined and then rewrapped; and their only child, my husband, was driven to some spot or other on the Bowery and instructed to give his presents away. Christian virtue, Mr. Fox. Give his presents to the less fortunate. He never had a Christmas present in his life, and he was probably, when he was ten, worth that many in millions in trust funds alone. Do you understand? To Mrs. Sifford, you had to be Jesus Christ to deserve that much money, but my husband wasn't Jesus Christ, and knew it. He knew he had the money and didn't deserve it. He was locked into a box and tried to drink his way out."

"I see," Fox said.

"Thirteen years ago, it was particularly bad. I've no idea what was happening. All I know is that Mrs. Sifford parked her son up here, in the old house, in the care of Mr. Marsiglia, who was the general manager of the estate. The old man could not control him. So they brought me in."

It all fell into place for Fox. He understood the particular professional tone. Mrs. Sifford was a nurse. And a damn good one.

"You did a good job," Fox said.

"He is a very nice, decent man. And I didn't marry him for his money."

"I never thought you did," Fox said.

"Of course you did," she said. "What else would you think? But it doesn't matter. I don't even think the three million matters."

It probably didn't to her, Fox thought. She was living on the idea that her job was complete. How long had it taken her, Fox wondered, to straighten out her husband, then straighten out the old house, and finally get it all to the point where they were actually living? More than living: planning, doing things. Like the trees in the field. He took another broad look at her, and thought: maybe she's scared. She doesn't want to go through any of that again. Like the relationship between the old and new in this house, everything was in precarious balance.

"The problem is," Fox said, "it matters to the estate."

"The estate is not a person," Mrs. Sifford said. "And I am only interested in people."

Not exactly a person, Fox thought, but almost one, a real legal entity, like a ghost person, with the power to sign checks and authorize actions of all sorts, with the power of the courts behind it, and with demands placed on it and summarized in laws and rules. Until the estate was wound up, finally stamped with the seal of approval of a probate court, it was real and could sue and be sued. It talked through Fox. But she was right. And I do, goddamn it, think of estates as if they were real people, Fox realized. What's wrong with me?

"Has your husband ever received any communication from his father?" Fox asked.

"No. Does it matter?"

"Mrs. Sifford might have given the money to him, to sort of buy him off, to get him out of her life."

"I suppose anything is possible," the woman said. "If she did, she was foolish. You can't buy people off. They always come back. And you can't drink them away either. Everything shows up in the final tally."

Which was exactly how Kim Hartman looked at things, Fox thought, thinking that there was some psychic link between these two women, both of them coming from different backgrounds, but convecting anyway.

And Fox was *right*. There was a psychic link between the two women. For a moment, Fox had almost grasped an idea that might save his life. But he didn't quite make it. And Mrs. Sifford, who had problems of her own, did not help him, even though she was a very good nurse.

"Before his mother sent Mr. Sifford up here, he lived at the house?" Fox continued.

"His wife, his first wife, had thrown him out. For good reason. She was in the process of divorcing him. Yes, he lived at the Sifford town house. And I'm sure what he said is true: he can't remember signing anything, but he probably did. But you can check all of that out, can't you, Mr. Fox? You have experts."

"It seems he did cosign the mortgage note."

"Then he did," the woman said. "My husband has come a long way. And, frankly, I really don't want him to remember what happened thirteen years ago, and I don't think he does. He ought to get some benefit from all the time he spent trying to kill himself with a bottle. I'm tired too. Not like him, who I insist take a nap every afternoon. I mean, my mind is tired. I need to get outside."

19

THEY WENT outside. The sun was now directly overhead, but it was not hot. The wind, cooled on the big river, roared over the big mountain.

"When I'm tired, I have a little walk." She meant a walk in both senses of the word. They were on a path that circled behind the house. The top of the path was mossy, and soft, and the sides of the walk were carefully built up with stone walls.

"He had men build these walks all over the mountain," she went on, talking about old Baron Meecham. "Can you imagine how much time it took to build these stone walls, how many men it took? Look at this."

They had come to a turn in the path and at the turn there was an ornately carved stone bench, facing the view.

"The carvings are great," Fox said, looking at it.

"The exedra?" Mrs. Sifford said. "Old Mr. Meecham had hundreds of these exedras built all over the place, and up on top of the mountain, he put up an oracle. Lots of these exedras are set in the path up to the oracle, so you can rest on the way."

So these stone benches are called exedras, Fox thought. Interesting. He wondered what an oracle looked like.

"Mr. Fox, don't miss the forest for the trees," Mrs. Sifford said. "The whole point of the design is the view."

It was some view. It was the view in the Church painting Fox had seen at the Sifford town house. The only thing missing was the exploding sunset that Church had thrown over the big river. But here were his four mountains: Storm King, Bull Hill, Crow's Nest, and Breakneck. Like a huge gate, with the river squeezed through it. You could see why Henry Hudson had gone on. A gigantic gate like this had to lead somewhere spectacular. Poor Hudson, Fox thought, the river just went to awful Albany.

"You live in a spectacularly beautiful place," Fox said.

She kept going along the path again after pausing to look at the spectacle, moving quickly as if she'd lived here long enough to memorize it. They turned another corner, and the path had led them in a circle, right back to the house itself, and to his car.

"I feel much better," she said, and held out her hand for Fox to shake. She shook his firmly.

"It's possible that the money may turn up, along with your father-in-law," Fox said. "But it is also possible that the money was invested with Marsiglia.

The builder. I may actually have to sue him in order to get some information.''

"Mr. Fox," she said firmly, "I have no doubt that your Marsiglia can take care of himself. Deal with him any way you want. But make sure that none of this comes back to haunt us, or touches our Marsiglia. Do you understand?"

"I'll try to do things quietly," Fox said.

"Protect us, Mr. Fox. That's your job."

She turned and went back into the house, leaving Fox at his car. She trudged determinedly in her red tennis shoes, looking like the women they use now in commercials: honest, plain, down-to-earth. She trudged back into what had been the Meecham "country place," which, though it had lost three floors, was still huge and baronial. She left the massive door open, the way Fox had found it. As if she were living in some small community of tract houses, where everyone knew everyone else and hung their clothes on the line and talked over their back fence. Another open door, another open invitation to visit, just like Gauder's always open office door.

20

As THEY drove home, it began to rain. The parkway they had chosen had been built at a time when cars ambled along at about forty and the people of the city drove out on a sunny day, looking at the trees that lined the road. Now, in this surging downpour, fast station wagons sloshed along the parkway at sixty.

The speeding wagons usually had dogs in them. And the beasts had their silly heads out the windows, even in the rainstorm, hanging their tongues out, as if they wanted to catch the water.

Don't these people care about the children in their cars? Fox wondered.

"What's the matter?"

"The rain."

"You'll get me through," Kim Hartman said. "You're my highwayman. You take me to the Ardeonuig Hotel and give me pearls. There's a sneaky illicit quality to you." She snuggled against Fox.

Highwayman, Fox thought, remembering the poem his mother had taught him when he was very young:

The highwayman came riding—riding—riding
The highwayman came riding, up to the old inn-door.

How did the poem go? And who should be waiting there?

> The landlord's black-eyed daughter,
> Bess, the landlord's daughter...

Who was in love with the highwayman. Then didn't the police come, or something? Or was it the king's men, patrolling the highway and trying to catch the highwayman. Yes, Fox thought, the king's men came.

Fox's car climbed a steep hill. A red station wagon was at the crest. It seemed to drop off the other side.

What had Bess, the black-eyed daughter, done? The king's men tied a musket to her, with the barrel under her chin, trying to keep her quiet. And Bess wiggled one of her little fingers free, reached the trigger, and blew her brains out, warning the highwayman.

Why do I *always* remember that poem?

And then what happened to the highwayman? Oh yes, Fox thought, remembering all of it now, but not the exact text: when the highwayman heard about Bess, he rode back. To kill the king's men. Hundreds of them. They shot him down like a dog in the moonlight. Am I a highwayman? Fox wondered. Or is Marsiglia?

The red station wagon was a highwayman, skidding dangerously, still on the road, still going down the hill, but sliding sideways.

"You've been so nice," Kim said sleepily. "I'm going to get you a special present."

Fox came to rigid attention, his hands clenched on the wheels, his back ramrod straight. The red station wagon in front of them was skidding sideways, taking up both lanes, decelerating at the same time. Fox didn't answer. Kim sat up and saw in an instant what the situation was. She grabbed Fox's arm.

He tried to bring his car under control, slowing it, pumping delicately on the brake pedal. What was worse? Hitting the car or the trees? The car, Fox thought, it's moving. All right. Hit the red car if you have to, and not the trees.

Down at the bottom of the hill, there was a small lake in the middle of the road. That goddamned red wagon is going to hit the lake, Fox thought, and who the hell knows which way he's going then? Into the trees? Over the divider? Don't pump too hard. Don't skid yourself. Seat belt on.

"Seat belt," Fox yelled. Kim's wasn't on.

Kim Hartman didn't move. She just clutched Fox's arm tighter.

The red car hit the lake. It skated into a tree. It hit hard, the rear end of the car sticking out into the slow lane. I've got time, Fox thought, if I don't skid too. What the hell will the lake do to me? He eased into the fast lane, to get by the red car. The goddamned idiots are beginning to get out of the car, Jesus Christ, Fox suddenly realized, and began honking. How the hell do they survive, he wondered? They were walking around the car. Their goddamned red retriever was leaping around right in the middle of the fast lane lake. Good-bye dog, Fox thought.

He had gotten his speed down to around thirty-five. But it had taken some time. The water ran down the hill, into the parkway lake, and Fox had to be very careful. Oh, Christ, he thought, can't they hear me? The goddamned idiot wants to see what kind of shape his car is in. Is he stunned or something? Oh, Christ, he's trying to get the dog. Hell, he's trying to catch his dog.

"*Kill him,*" Kim Hartman said, "*not us.*" She said it in a level, straight tone as if she were a general issuing an order to a private. But it was unnecessary: Fox had already made the decision. Good-bye dog, Fox thought, good-bye man. I love Kim Hartman. The man had gotten the dog by the collar. Fox hit the lake. The water flooded the windshield. His car skidded, then righted itself on the other side of the lake.

Why are they so lucky? Fox wondered, knowing that if he'd killed the man, he would have felt it. He had hit a deer once, on a fishing trip, and it had broken Fox's radiator—and this on a back road, far into the woods, when he had been traveling very slowly.

"Lord," Kim Hartman said, "please take over and get us to the city."

21

THE LORD got them to New York, but not into the same apartment. Kim Hartman thought it would be "more sensible" for them to spend the night separately, and "tidy up" their individual apartments. Fox said yes.

That was a mistake. Fox was usually doggedly determined about Kim Hartman. Maybe the drive down had tired him out. Fox had gotten this far with Kim Hartman only because he had pursued her like a man obsessed. But now, tired and losing his mind, he made a mistake and said yes to a separation.

He did not sleep at all that night. It didn't have to do with the accident, or Kim Hartman, or the Sifford matter. He had one of his seizures of self-loathing.

They came with increasing regularity. He used Scotch and lots of it and, finally, at around four in the morning he would be staggering around his apartment and would collapse somewhere, on the rug or sofa, but still not asleep. Still cursing himself.

Tonight he told himself that this was what Charles Sifford, Jr., had done every night, and did he want to end up that way? Puttering around planting trees? Fox cursed himself the way some demented father might have if his son had not met his expectations. And look at Charles Sifford now, Fox swore, thirteen years married to a nurse and living like a zombie.

Fox did not realize that Charles Sifford, Jr., had made it, was making it, and that he, Fox, was not. Fox believed that because he cursed himself out and got drunk, he would somehow change in the morning.

Charles Sifford, Jr., had gotten very, very lucky, finding this particular nurse who loved him. Robert Fox had not gotten that lucky. Kim Hartman was wonderful all right, and good for Fox, but she was not a princess in a fairy tale. Her kiss could not turn a frog into a prince. In fact, her kiss, given at the wrong time, in the wrong place, might turn Fox into a lunatic.

Fox lay staring at the dark leather sofa he had inherited. This lawyer, who absolutely never drank at lunch, and usually only had wine at dinner, lay staring at the sofa, wondering if he could make it over to it. He tried to pull himself along the old red living room rug, the whole apartment blurring now. The ancient, puckered law degrees of his father. The painting of his mother. The old books. All blurred. The gray light of morning beginning to come in the window.

Let me sleep. Let me make it to the sofa.

And now, the telephone began to ring. The powerful old black phone sounded out its whacking bell from the old telephone room, and Fox switched direction. He tried to crawl toward the hall. He tried to stand, fell over on his back, and tried again.

It just kept ringing, ringing. It would not stop. He dug his fingers into the rug. He was trying to get to her. And he could not. His mind was going, literally feeling as if it would leave his body to get to that ringing phone. Good-bye Fox, his mind seemed to say to him.

Mother, Fox thought. God, Mother, Father, help me.

And the ringing stopped. He was asleep.

PART THREE

Broadmoor

22

THE SIFFORD matter was not the only work Fox had. He had inherited, from Gauder, many, many matters. Moreover, the senior partner in Fox's firm, Richard Lovett, fought violently against making any of the young associate lawyers into partners. He liked to fire people, and hated to pay them. So even more work landed on Fox's desk.

Gauder had trained Fox to be very efficient. But Fox was beginning to ignore some of that training and do his work in an odd way. He devoted most of his time to the Sifford matter because Kim Hartman was involved in it. Because Kim Hartman was working at the Sifford town house, Fox also devoted himself to other matters if they happened to bring him near the town house. Then he could drop in on Kim.

Money was not an issue. Billable hours were not

taken into consideration. Fox no longer thought much about the good of the firm or his take from the general partnership. He meditated, got prodded by his secretary, Miss Algur, and went on errands messengers should have run, if the errands got him anywhere near Kim.

Of course, this surprised several clients. The president of Bagnall Industries, whose office was only three blocks away, did not get his will drawn up. But Janet Poppin, who was a maid, got hers done for free. She happened to be employed by another client of Fox's, who happened to have a large apartment near the town house.

Fortunately, the other partners in Fox's firm were all egomaniacs concerned exclusively with their own problems. If Richard Lovett, for example, had stopped jetting off to California to "make deals," if he had even stopped firing young associate lawyers for a few days, or complaining about the fact that old Gauder still had an office, he might have noticed what Fox was doing. Eventually, of course, he would notice. Time was running out for Fox.

"How do you do?" Fluffy Ravenel said. Fox had decided to "drop in" on the Sifford town house, because he had invented some important meeting right around the corner. "Mrs. Hartman has told me so much about you."

Fluffy Ravenel had black hair that came just to her shoulders and was tied back with a ribbon. She was wearing gold circle earrings and had the bazoomas that Kim Hartman had been deprived of. She also had a red leather shoulder bag. Where she packs her rod, Fox thought. The girl stuck her hand out, gave

Fox a great big smile, and explained that Kim Hartman wasn't there.

"Well," Fox said, "nice to meet you."

He turned to go.

"Do you have family in Savannah?" Fluffy asked. She had kept her Southern accent. She didn't say *family,* just *famly.*

"No."

"Any cousins in Middleburg?" Fluffy said.

"No, I don't," Fox said, and began to wonder about the girl. How had she survived Radcliffe? Probably on pure energy. Racing through like a bullet, so that the place had no effect on her whatsoever. She was a fast girl, and because of it, still pure Southern.

"One more thing, Mr. Fox," Fluffy said. "Let's go."

Go? "Where?" he said.

"Up these beautifully carved stairs," Fluffy said and smiled. "Up into the bedroom."

Fox instinctively jumped back. Bedroom? The girl was mad.

"Mrs. Hartman asked me to show you something," Fluffy said quickly. "And, Mr. Fox, we cannot disappoint her."

Now that was the right tack to take with Fox. He headed up the beautiful staircase. On each of the landings, there were pictures—some of them the work of Frederick Church—in which the sun was always setting or rising, always exploding over something: jungle clearings, icebergs, river valleys.

"Where *do* you come from?" Fluffy asked as they climbed.

"New York."

"New York? You mean you were *born* here?"

"Right," Fox said.

"Well that is interesting. Very interesting. You are a native. Well."

Interesting? It would be awfully easy to strike up a conversation with Fluffy in a bar, Fox thought. Then some man would probably get the wrong impression and make the wrong move and get plugged. Fox did not realize that in Fluffy's crowd, in the group that included people like Jackson and other young men and women of New York City, it *was* surprising to meet a "native." This was where the young people came to launch their careers. For them, New York was Boom Town City bursting with opportunity, high paying jobs, and good bars.

"Maybe you know the Buckleys," Fluffy chattered. "Some of them are from New York, but they winter in Pickens. My daddy loves them. And he's a lawyer too."

Fox had no idea what Fluffy was talking about. He didn't realize that Pickens was in South Carolina, and that it just isn't that big a state.

Feeling peevish, Fox said, "Exactly where are we going, Fluffy?" There were a lot of bedrooms in the Sifford town house. The whole point of the trip was to see Kim Hartman, not the female equivalent of Jackson.

"The master bedroom, filled with exactly sixty-seven pieces of art, silver, and various goodies,"

Fluffy said. "Which I would estimate in value at about two hundred thousand dolleros."

All right, Fox thought, we'll call them dolleros. Why not? Let her have her enthusiasm, let her be into her job. Call them dolleros, and ask where I'm born, you toss your head, and be totally unselfconscious about your tremendous-looking chest. Be young. Let her stay up all night dancing. He couldn't fight the energy.

"Which bedroom, Mr. Fox, has not been used for lo these many years. Mrs. Sifford slept one floor up."

With that, she threw open the door to the dark room. There was a huge magnificent bed, with a deeply carved swirling headboard. Large wooden birds were perched on the bedposts.

"How do you know she didn't sleep here?"

"You sleep with your jewels," Fluffy said. "You sleep with your gear. If you know what I mean. Your stuff, your things. Right?"

"Right," Fox said.

"Especially if you're ninety-four and can't truck around too fast."

Fluffy went over to a bureau, pulled open a drawer, and kept pulling it. Then she held it like a box, her clipboard under her arm, and put it on the bed.

"Speaking of gear," she said, poking around in the drawer. "You will find, here, a few relics of our Mr. Sifford. Not much. No clothes. But there's this." She held up a gold watch that dangled from a gold chain. "And this." It was a money clip, also gold, with the initials C.F.S. on it. "And some more of these personal trinkets. Gold. All from Tiffany's, and very, very nice. All right?''

"All right," Fox said.

"Why didn't he take them with him? Ask yourself that, Mr. Fox.''

Yes, Fox thought, Fluffy's got the mind of a girl who keeps a gun. And can probably use it. And really is not so dumb, she just looks that way. She may pack a rod, but she's not going to indiscriminately pump four slugs into a lout who mauls her. Ask yourself, he thought, but not here.

As he left, Fluffy stuck her hand out again, and insisted on a vigorous Southern shake: "Y'all come back, hear!''

23

"I SAW YOUR button light up," stern Miss Algur said to Fox from the door. "I assume you are about to do some work without explaining it to me, so that I could not record it in your office diary."

Come on, Fox thought, give me a break.

"If you have to know, I'm trying to order some food, Algur," Fox snapped. "I may be a partner, but I do my own cooking. Did you barge in to suggest a menu?''

"Mr. Fox," she said, glaring, "it is because you

have given me standing instructions to always put through Mrs. Hartman's calls. She is on the other line. Should I hang up on her?''

Mrs. Hartman? Fox was already punching buttons, and his empty icebox faded into the background along with Algur.

''Your timing is bad,'' Kim Hartman said. ''I got back five minutes after you left. What did you think?''

What are we doing tonight? he thought.

''Fox,'' Kim said, ''listen to me. Fluffy says I'm going to find a body in the attic. Am I? Fluffy says when a man leaves, he takes his watch. I can't take a body, Fox.''

''No bodies,'' Fox promised.

''Well, why didn't he take his watch?'' Kim asked. Fox switched the phone to his other ear. He swiveled his chair and put his feet up on the sill.

''He probably didn't take the watch because she wouldn't let him. Probably because it was a gift from her. Something like that.''

''Fluffy is looking for bullet holes behind the pictures. She wants to go down into the cellar.''

''Tell her to stick to art.''

''I don't know, Fox. It's not a good day. I don't like this old house. People do kill themselves, Fox, and they kill other people, and this town house has a thousand nooks and crannies, and closets. God, closets. Fluffy's got me believing that a skeleton is going to fall out of one. Fluffy's so excited about it that she wants to work through the night. She wants to work through the night and look for skeletons.''

"There aren't any skeletons," Fox said.

"Why don't I believe you?" she said. "Why is it you don't comfort me?"

"Where's my present?" Fox said. "The surprise I was supposed to get because of the pearls I gave you."

"All you think about is yourself."

"Is this some sort of crank call?"

"What's the matter with you, Fox?"

"Actually, I was just thinking that we ought to run away. Why don't we run away?"

"We just did. Last weekend."

"It felt good," Fox said. "Let's do it again."

"Robert is coming."

"Fluffy can take care of him," Fox said, and smiled to himself. Fluffy would give the kid something to think about. Fluffy is probably just what Robert needs. Robert was seventeen. He needed an older woman. The way Fox did.

"Actually, maybe he's going to his father's. I don't know, Fox, I'm losing my mind. I'm talking too much. I'm beginning to feel like a New York mumbler. Is this the way it starts? Will I end up walking the streets, mumbling and grumbling with imaginary people?"

"Fluffy's just got you unhinged."

"You're right. Why did I hire her?"

"Because she looks just the way your mother wanted you to look."

"You're right, that's it. I'm sick. I need a shrink

again. Fluffy was sent to haunt me with my failures of the past. It all comes back. And Mr. Sifford will. Only he'll come back dead.''

"He's not there," Fox said. "I promise."

"How could you possibly know?"

"Don't worry about skeletons."

"Fox, I can't have dinner. You can't spend the night. This is a crank call. I'm sorry, very sorry."

She hung up without saying good-bye. She did that all the time. She'd called Fox because she was scared and she'd turned instinctively to the person she loved, which, unfortunately, Fox did not understand.

24

No DINNER with Kim Hartman? In a mood of resignation and despair, Fox called in Miss Algur.

"Algur," Fox said, "what is most pressing?"

"*Miss* Algur!" She stamped out of the office and came back with a file, which she slammed down on his desk.

"I am sorry, Miss Algur," Fox said. "I don't know what's wrong with me today."

Miss Algur's eyes rolled toward the ceiling. Fox didn't know what was wrong with him today? It was every day as far as Algur was concerned.

"Mr. Fox," she said, "I have no idea what is the

most pressing at this point. But that file is eight months old.'' She shook her head.

Algur really is getting sort of loony, Fox thought, maybe it's time for her to retire. He picked up the file and began to get down to work.

The file concerned a man who wanted to give away a Monet painting appraised at one million seven hundred and seventy-five thousand dollars. The man did not want to pay any taxes. He didn't give a damn about art, he just wanted his children and grandchildren to get the equity. Fox worked on this problem for a while. Reasoning that in fact a painting was no different for tax purposes than a piece of real estate, he decided that the old man could give his children and grandchildren pieces of the painting, the way you can give away pieces of a field. He sent Jackson into the library to do a little research. The research showed that no one had ever tried to give away a tangible work of art in that way. So Fox decided to go ahead. The analogy was clear. It would certainly give the IRS something to think about. In fact, it did give the IRS something to think about, and the painting became the basis of a law suit, and later Fox would argue that law suit in the Supreme Court and win it. All this would take seven years and the man would be long since dead. All this would happen because Kim Hartman had not had dinner with Fox, and had made him angry and therefore creative.

It was dark now and perfect Jackson stood at the door.

"Is there anything else you'd like me to do?" he said.

He stood in his dark suit, his hands clasped behind his back, suit jacket buttoned, tie unwrinkled, looking as if he'd not yet worked that day and was ready to put in an all-nighter.

"I'm going to surprise you, Jackson," Fox said. "I'm going to take you to dinner. Are you surprised?"

"No, sir," Jackson said. He's turning a little surly, Fox thought, there's something in his tone. Have I been too rude to him? And he vowed that tonight he would try to be nice to Jackson.

"Did you have other plans?" Fox said, politely. "Is this inconvenient?"

"My plans are always subject to the requirements of the firm," Jackson stated.

"No they're not," Fox snapped. Jackson was too much, he thought. "They are not subject to the requirements of anybody. I'm smart enough to know that. I see your little tumblers spinning in your big bank mind."

Why did I let that go? Fox wondered. I am angry. Is it all Kim Hartman? "We're going to eat together, Jackson," Fox said, "and neither of us is going to give the other any crap."

Fox geared up. That was how he thought about it: getting his gear together as if he were going fishing. He put on his coat, and patted the pockets, making sure that everything was in place. I am not like Jackson, Fox thought, he probably knows by extrasensory perception that his notebook is in one breast pocket, his wallet in the other, and his pen in the vest. Then he went down in the elevator with Jackson and walked out into the street. It was about seven and the streets were deserted. Pages of the *New York Post* rolled down Wall like tumbleweeds. Without any people, the big buildings seemed somehow lonely to Fox. Or is that just me? Fox wondered.

"We're going to do it all tonight, Jackson," Fox said. "I'm not taking you to a stodgy club. We're going to get away from this street. I have made a special reservation."

To get away, they walked over to the World Trade Center, shot up in the fast-moving elevators, and sat down at Windows on the World. Fox ordered for both of them to make sure that Jackson would get a big fat healthy meal and not—"for the good of the firm"— decide that he should eat a hot dog and save some money. Fox also ordered the very best in wine.

"You didn't touch your wine," Fox said. He had already drunk half the bottle and dinner hadn't come yet.

"No," Jackson said.

"You didn't sample it."

Jackson said nothing.

"Are you a Mormon?" Fox asked.

Jackson shook his head.

"Then, is this supposed to impress me? Or are you a member of some weird perfect boy club? Did all of you take a vow at fourteen that you would never touch liquor until one of you had been elected president of the United States? Or sat on the Supreme Court?"

Fox had drunk the half bottle, and it was indeed good wine. Now he was buzzing, angry that Jackson seemed to function just like a telephone answering machine. Telephone answering machines, Fox thought: technology that always gives you a bum message.

"Am I supposed to believe that because you don't drink wine at dinner or smoke or lie you're the perfect lawyer?" Fox leaned forward. "I already know you're the perfect lawyer, Jackson, I just want to know you're human. Are you?"

Jackson's face twitched. Fox did not notice it. But he realized he'd gone too far, and tried to save himself the only way he knew how. That was to talk shop. So he gave Jackson an overview of the whole Sifford matter, telling him even about Fluffy, and the watch, and the bed, and his trip up the Hudson, and then, as nicely as he could, he said, "What do you think?"

"Am I supposed to?" Jackson said.

I really did go too far, Fox thought. I behaved like a damn idiot, and he's right.

"I am sorry, Jackson," Fox said.

Jackson said nothing. You could not read any expression on his face.

"I'm sorry," Fox pleaded. "I know you're human, and yes, I really want to know what you think. You're smart. Jackson, I'll behave myself. All right?"

No expression: nothing from Jackson.

"Jackson, what do I have to do? I'm wrong. You're right. I've made an ass out of myself."

The wine had done it to Fox. There was no stopping him. He was either angry or maudlin. "You set off something inside me. I don't know exactly how you do it. But it's my problem, not yours. Are you worried about partnership? Are you worried what I'd do? Jackson, listen, about partnership, all that matters is the work. Now forgive me. Have some wine."

Jackson's arms were folded across his chest, and he had that expression of indecision moving toward quick resolution that Fox had seen on the faces of a hundred judges. The verdict came down. In favor of Fox.

"I would if I had any stomach."

"What?" Fox said.

"If I hadn't had half of it taken out."

My God, Fox thought, no stomach. Bleeding ulcers at twenty-five? Is that what it costs to be perfect?

"I'll make an exception tonight," Jackson said suddenly. And he picked up his glass, draining the entire thing, and filling it again. He shook his head. "You know," he said, "working for you is hell."

25

"JACKSON," FOX SAID, "are you sure that's all right?" They were on their second bottle of wine, and Jackson was certainly pumping a lot of it into what was left of his stomach.

"If you're going to do it, do it," Jackson said. "I think I can get away with it. If not, you'll know."

"Know what?" Fox asked.

"The details."

"What details?"

"Concerning how I clutch my stomach and begin rolling all over the floor embarrassing you terribly at Windows on the World."

Fox was worried about Jackson's stomach, but hadn't noticed that Jackson was drunk. Fox was pondering, wondering about changes. When he'd gone to law school, you didn't have to be perfect to get in, you didn't have to be perfect to get a job in a good law firm, or make partner. That was twelve years ago. Now there were too many law schools, too many lawyers, and therefore too much competition.

"Is your stomach really that bad?" Fox asked.

"Usually." Even so, Jackson picked up his glass and drained it again. "Now here's how I see it. Start with the bed. That's where Mrs. Banning was with Mrs. Sifford, right?''

"Right," Fox said, who was also feeling the effects of the second bottle.

"Wrong," Jackson answered. "Mrs. Sifford wasn't in bed with Mrs. Banning. Sorry. I am drunk. Mrs. Sifford was a religious fanatic. She wasn't into that. It was Mr. Sifford with Banning in bed. That's what I mean. And in pops Mrs. Sifford at the wrong time. So, out goes Mrs. Banning. Did Mrs. Sifford shoot or otherwise eliminate her husband? No, because Mrs. Banning is still alive, and the wife would have offed both of them at once . . ."

Offed? Fox thought. What a mind Jackson has. He and Fluffy would make quite a pair.

". . . in a crime of passion. Right? Did I get that right? I mean, if she caught both of them in bed together, she would have plugged them both at once, if she was going to. But she didn't. So maybe the money did go to pay off the husband and get him out of her life."

"And Marsiglia?"

"He got a lot of money, all at once, just when he needed it. So maybe Mrs. Sifford let Mrs. Banning go, then killed her husband, and Marsiglia helped her out, for three million two. Possible. I don't know. Why is Marsiglia so quiet about all of this? Why won't he talk to you? Maybe Mrs. Sifford paid Marsiglia to off her husband. And maybe the price was three million two."

"Jackson, you have a disgusting mind," Fox said.

"Thanks," Jackson said, raising his glass.

"Horrible, but intelligent."

"Or maybe Mrs. Sifford paid off the husband to get him out of her life. Then Mrs. Banning, with the help of Marsiglia, wasted him and took the three million two in going-away money. How's that? She did invest some with him. Maybe she's lying and she actually invested more, through all those other little companies we don't know anything about. See what I mean?"

"How the hell will we ever find out?" Fox asked.

"I don't know, you're the partner," Jackson said. "There's also Gladney."

"Gladney?"

"He's your friend, not mine. I'm just a slave associate. I look around and see people like . . ." He paused. "From my point of view none of you looks completely balanced. What about Gladney? Do you really believe that he didn't watch old Mrs. Sifford like a hawk? All right. She owned a building outright, mortgagable at any time. Gladney told her that she ought to sign some little tax form. Only it wasn't a tax form. It was the mortgage. He was right there the whole time. He had all the information. Why couldn't he have done it? Maybe he does it all the time. It's a neat scheme.

"Anyway, that would be nice for you. Gladney is your friend. If it's Marsiglia, and say he really did eliminate Mr. Sifford, why wouldn't he eliminate you? Think about this: think about all the office buildings and apartment buildings he owns. And all those people who work for him, wearing their little uniforms who so politely escort you into the elevator or open the door. Only when they open the door to the elevator it turns out that the cage hasn't arrived yet. You get to free-fall. How many times do you look to make sure it's actually there when you get in? How many office buildings does Marsiglia own? How many elevators?"

"Please, Jackson," Fox said. "Take it easy."

"Cheer up. Maybe the husband will walk in the door tomorrow with a really deep tan after spending thirteen years in the Bahamas. In a very oblique way, he'll explain that he had been away because of a slight disagreement with his devoted wife. So then, your only problem will be the gift taxes on the three million. They would be a liability to the estate. By the way, how are you going to handle this?"

"Quietly," Fox whispered.

26

"SOMEONE'S WORKING late," Jackson said. They were standing at the window, about to leave, looking across the island of Manhattan at their office building. On the floor below the one occupied by their firm, all the lights were on: the night gnomes, nocturnal dwarfs, had come out. And indeed, many of the cleaning personnel were. The ones who like to work through the night and sleep through the day often did have something wrong with them. A scalded face, red and twisted. A hunched back. Some reason for avoiding the day.

Often, when Fox had been working late, he had been shocked to see some deformed man unexpectedly flash by the open door of his office, the vacuum cleaner dragging, rattling behind him like long leg irons, the man limping with, say, a clubfoot or bent over with a hunched back. They would flash by Fox's open door, not wanting to be seen, probably feeling that their special territory had been violated: what are you doing here, their faces seemed to say to Fox. Night is ours, it belongs to the crazy, the twisted, the weird.

"See what I mean?" Jackson said. On their floor, it was dark, except for one window.

"Yes," Fox looked at his watch. Twelve. He had spent a lot of time with Jackson, Fox realized, but at least Jackson seemed to be in a better mood. Fox felt good about helping Jackson: you had to. It was part of the responsibility of being a partner. And Jackson seems more human to me, too, Fox thought. It's going to be easier working with him. Now, when Jackson suddenly walked into Fox's office to announce that he was leaving to become chief counsel to some Senate committee, Fox realized that he might actually miss Jackson. It was too bad Jackson had no intention of staying with the firm. He was a fast boy all right, even though he had proved to be human.

Fox had telephoned ahead because it was impossible to find a cab on Wall Street at this hour, or any hour after eight. The only humans were the old men and women sleeping, twisted under newspapers, in the empty, sheltering arches of the bank entrances.

Their cab was waiting, Jackson stepped back to let the partner in first.

"Jackson, this one's just for you," Fox said.

"Why?"

"I'm heading back to the firm."

"Listen, if there's some work . . ." Jackson said.

"Not your kind," Fox said. "Good night. Sweet dreams."

Jackson got into the cab. Shaking his head and thanking Fox, he disappeared into the night.

Fox met no gnomes in the empty office building. He knew the corridors of his firm so well that he didn't even bother to turn on any lights. He came around the corner, to the little office, and opened the door. Gauder lay with his head on his desk blotter, snoring. The cleaning people had just cleaned right around him: his office was immaculate. Does it really make any difference if he sleeps here at the firm, or back in his apartment? Fox wondered. I could leave him if I had a blanket. Or I could put my coat over him.

Fox sat down in the chair. Gauder snored. This firm is my family, Fox thought, and Gauder is like an old father that I've got to take care of. He trained me and now I handle him the way he handled me when I first came to this firm: like a child. Gauder was a bachelor. A long time ago, he'd become married to the firm. Now the goddamn firm has a responsibility to take care of him, Fox thought. Why do they want to take away his tiny office? Why does everything get taken away? What's wrong with Lovett? Why does he single out Gauder? This firm can afford to break some rules about things like retirement. Gauder never broke a rule, Fox thought, then realized that Gauder's rules had been of a special kind.

Things are changing, Fox thought. Yes, Jackson is human all right and I like him, but would he take care of me if I were in Gauder's situation? *No.* Jackson is going to marry someone like Fluffy and have five perfect children. That, in the end, will be his family. And besides, Jackson won't even be here. He'll be in the White House, nursing his ulcers.

Kim Hartman's got to marry me, Fox thought. Otherwise I'm headed for Broadmoor, with nurses who pat you on the head with washcloths, polishing your old, bald scalp. Gauder's head looked polished. Maybe one of the cleaning gnomes had mistaken him for a piece of furniture, sprayed his dome with Lemon Pledge, and given him a chamois cloth shine.

I'm tired, Fox thought. I could put my feet up on this desk, lean back in this chair and go to sleep, too. Then when Gauder woke up in the morning, I could tell him that we had worked together all night. It had been an emergency, so the firm had called on him. Gauder would probably believe me, too. We put in a lot of all-nighters together. At sixty, and a senior partner, Gauder had been strong as a boy. At seventy, he was completely senile. You go fast, Fox thought.

Everything goes fast. You make plans, and something unexpected interrupts them. People die on you. My timing is always off, Fox thought. I had better timing when I was working for Gauder, when the old man was in his prime. The old man could sure move at sixty.

Those all-nighters. And he could think too, and work out difficult problems, and come up with unexpected solutions. You had to come up with unexpected solutions to difficult problems, because people were wacky, and sometimes it seemed to Fox that the more money the people had, the wackier they were. Money seemed to allow them all kinds of strange behavior.

Fox remembered the shipping deal he had worked on with Gauder, when Fox had been Jackson's age. The client had inherited several millions. The client's father had been a shipping tycoon. So the client decided he would be one, too. He put his money into ships. He flew out to exotic oriental places and went into partnership with men who wore diamonds on their little fingers and had gold teeth. Then the client died. A man's word is his bond: that was what the client had believed. His rich father had sent him to Groton. The rector had taught that a man's word is his bond. So the client never bothered to sign any contracts. His widow sat in Connecticut. His ships

plied the seas. But the partners with the gold teeth
said, Where are the contracts? A man's word is his
bond? Show it to us in writing. Until you do, those
ships are ours. This old man whose head now lay like
a polished gold ball on the blotter of his desk had
flown out to Singapore, Manila, Bangkok, Hong
Kong. And come back with signed contracts. Because he had played the partners against each other.
Come back with the contracts and the ships, and five
million dollars for the widow in Connecticut. Not
bad, Fox thought. Not bad at all.

How would Gauder have handled the Sifford situation? Fox wondered. By playing the partners against
each other until one cracked. And they were partners
all right: Mrs. Banning, Marsiglia, the missing Mr.
Sifford, even Gladney. Not partners in the sense that
they had necessarily plotted together, that each one
was guilty of some foul deed. But they were bonded
together just the same, connected by the money and
the memory of Belinda Meecham Sifford, frozen in a
quadrangle that cut across age or personal responsibility and was cemented by love and money. Connected in a web. And old Gauder would have begun
by playing them against each other. You pulled on
one, and that would tug on all the rest, and finally
everything would come out in the open. And Gauder
too would apply some selective pressure. Not with a
sledgehammer, but enough to make them worry.
There was one thing more, the most important of all.
He would play his hunches on the people. It had been
what Gauder did best, and what Fox would have to
do now. He knew them all. He even felt in some
strange way that he knew the missing Mr. Sifford. He

had formed impressions and suspicions, and he had hunches. He knew a lot, if he let his own hunches go. And one hunch was this: that somehow, in some way, either that money had indeed gone with the missing Mr. Sifford or it had ended up in the Blagden Building, financing Marsiglia's first venture. Which is *not* to say that Marsiglia stole the money, Fox reminded himself. But there is a way things happen in New York. There is a cycle. Old money becomes new money, old families retreat and retrench and new ones come forth. How is it done? The money is the trick. It is somehow passed along. It is the torch, passed from hand to hand. And it went to the railroad baron, old Mr. Meecham, and he passed it to his family, until they became old and dropped it—the money torch could burn you too, it was hard to hold—and then it was picked up by other surer hands who were ready to do something with it: build the new New York, like Marsiglia, the way old Mr. Meecham had built New York with his railroad. Either that, or Mr. Charles Sifford, Sr., was going to come walking in the door. That was possible, quite possible too, and that was one reason to play them against each other quietly. As Gauder would have done.

We are not detectives, Gauder had once lectured Fox. We don't go chasing around after people with guns and badges. We're thinkers, plotters, pushers, and pullers. We just let the tricky people trip themselves up. We are just good old-fashioned honest lawyers and very smart, Fox. Then Gauder had laughed. Sometimes, he'd said, you get a special case that takes you close to the beat of your own heart. And then we even have fun, Fox. Now get going. That was Gauder, Fox thought. Get going. But now, Gauder seemed to be going himself.

Well, it was time to get him home, but first Fox called the cab company, so that one would be waiting. Then he gently patted the old man's shoulder. Slowly he came awake, blinking like a newborn baby whose eyes could not take the light.

"Yes," Gauder said. "Yes?"

"Time to go home," Fox said.

"What time *is* it, Fox?"

"Twelve-thirty." Gauder rose up from his chair. His black suit hung in folds around his shriveled body. Where his shoulders had been, the suit seemed supported by thin twigs, so that it looked like black drapery.

"You know, Fox," Gauder said, "I forgot my damn watch today." He pointed a thin white finger at the bare spot on his wrist. "But I solved the Sifford matter."

"Really?" Fox said.

"Fox, who owns Sagamore Hill, Hyde Park, Jay's Homestead, Boscobel, and all the old palaces of Newport? The government or nonprofit corporations."

"Yes," Fox said.

"And the reason is taxes. How the hell can an ordinary man pay the taxes? He can't."

"Yes."

"So suppose you inherit some damn huge old mansion. Suppose it falls into your lap. And you want to keep it. What do you do?"

"I don't know," Fox said. "What?"

"You steal, damn it. Can't you see what I'm

125

getting at? You steal like your poor friend, the banker, Frederick Gladney.''

"What?''

"He inherited that huge old place, Red Bones, Blue Balls, Rock Bones—I can't keep the damn name straight. Don't remember what it's called. But he can't keep it up on a banker's salary. So he has to steal. From Mrs. Sifford. There you have it. There's the goddamn motive, Fox.''

"No,'' Fox said slowly. "Frederick Gladney sold off Red Rock.''

"Sold it?''

"It's just a bunch of tract houses now.''

"The whole damn place?''

"Yes,'' Fox said. "All subdivided.''

Gauder looked confused, as if logic, reason, had gotten lost somewhere in the dilapidated cobwebbed tunnels of his mind.

"Why did he sell?'' the old man mumbled.

"I guess for the reasons you've said. Taxes. Maintenance. His old family place is now called Red Rock Estates, and there are maybe a hundred houses on it. Gladney lives in town now.''

"I'll be damned,'' Gauder said. "And I had a hunch on this. I felt in my bones that Gladney took the money. Sorry, Fox. Don't listen to me. I'm too damn old to help. All sold? Fox, I don't know what the hell is happening anymore. Can't play my hunches. Don't listen to a man who can't tell time.''

Gauder tapped a thin white finger against the bare spot on his wrist.

"Let's go home,'' Fox said.

They headed into the dark corridor, moving

126

toward the elevator, Fox thinking about his friend Gladney, and losing track of Gauder. Up ahead of them were the new smoked-glass doors Richard Lovett had installed in Fox's firm. The old man walked right into them. Then fell down on the carpet.

Fox froze. Then he was down on the carpet beside Gauder, his arm around the old man. *They fall,* Fox thought, *they fall* and break their hips, and then they can't move. Then it all starts. And they die, the way my father did.

"Gauder!" Fox yelled.

"I'm all right," Gauder said. "But I did something wrong. What was it, Fox?"

I will kill Richard Lovett, Fox thought, I will shoot him in his chrome office. Nobody is going to hurt this man. Fox was drunk and the sight of Gauder on the floor, shrunken and looking confused, almost unhinged him.

"Help me, Fox."

Slowly, carefully, and with shaking hands, Fox got Gauder up on his feet, and then the Lord got them home.

27

THE ONLY time that Kim Hartman could not reach Fox was when he was in the bathroom, and Fox, if he ever became a senior partner in this firm, if he ever occupied the big founder's office which had glass windows on three sides and its own private bathroom, fully intended to have one put in there so that she could reach him then, too. Actually, Fox thought, there might already be a phone in there. Fox had never been in the bathroom in the senior partner's office. It was the one place in the firm he had never seen, and probably never would.

Richard Lovett had recently returned from a merger deal whose talks had been held in the Beverly Wilshire Hotel, and now he raved about California.

Maybe Lovett is going senile the way Gauder has, Fox thought. The Beverly Wilshire Hotel was a place Fox knew well. He had spent many hours there when he was a young associate and had been sent as the fourth man on some deals. There were telephones in the bathrooms of the Wilshire, even in the small rooms Fox had occupied. In the suites, they probably had them in the showers.

Maybe Lovett, California-crazied, *had* secretly put one in.

Then he thought: Why did I want to make partner so much? And why am I even thinking about being senior partner? I don't want it, and I'm not in a field where I'm going to make it. Some damn merger specialist will be the senior partner, and I don't care.

Kim Hartman's call was put through directly.

"Your Mr. Charles Sifford, Senior, is here," she said, reproachfully.

For a second Fox froze, and then he stood up at his desk, white-knuckling the phone. Back after thirteen years? Christ. Fox was so excited, for that instant, that he completely mistook the tone in Kim Hartman's voice.

"Back?"

"What do I do with him?" she said. "Call the police? The guard has already spanked him. Not exactly spanked. He's beaten him to a pulp."

"Slow down."

"Does the name Martin Beard mean anything to you?"

"What?"

"Martin Beard. That's his name. The guard took his wallet out of his pants. I mean took. He didn't bother to ask for it. He just ripped it out, pocket and all."

"I don't get it."

"Fox, you said no bodies. I almost jumped eight feet. I'm working away, dutifully cataloguing and appraising, and then there's this man, claiming it's all his, that he's Charles Sifford. Then the guard has him and is throttling him. Fluffy is here too, of course, and for one wild moment I thought: She will plug him."

"I'm sorry," Fox said.

"Actually Fluffy is quite calm. I'm not. Neither is Charles Sifford, or Martin Beard, or whatever you want to call him, and neither is the guard. He wants to call the police."

"No," Fox said. Gauder's rule: one never calls the police. "Is he sort of short, red haired, dirty looking?"

"Yes."

"Kim, he's a drunk old man who thinks he was Charles Sifford, because he's drunk up his brains. He was here, too. He's harmless."

"Well, he's toothless too. The guard managed to kick them down his throat. He was at your shop?"

"The nuts travel all over New York."

In the background, Fox heard some moaning. A lot of things turned over in his mind. Was Martin Beard harmless? Was he just a New York mumbler, talking to the air? The damn guard beat him to a pulp. Now Martin Beard *will* get some goddamned lawyer, who will take his case and will sue the estate for the beating. On tort grounds.

"Get him to an emergency room," he said.

"What? Who's supposed to take him? Me?"

"Not you. And definitely not the guard. I'll be there."

"And soon I hope." She hung up on Fox.

Fox didn't even bother to get his coat. He was halfway to his door when he realized Miss Algur was standing in it.

"Mr. Fox," she said, "you have a client waiting."

A client, Fox thought, so what? How does Algur know when I'm about to run out of the office? Is she listening in on my telephone calls?

"What client?"

"Mr. Storhang, the president of Bagnall Industries," Miss Algur said. "Need I remind you, Mr. Fox, that Bagnall Industries *and* its president are clients of the firm."

There was a tremor in Miss Algur's voice. When something goes wrong in law firms, they fire the secretary first, and give the partner a second, third, sometimes even a fourth chance.

"Please, Mr. Fox, please. I asked if I could arrange this appointment. He's been waiting for eight months to have his will drawn up. Now he's actually come to the firm. I told you all about this."

Had she? Fox really couldn't remember. He hesitated. It *was* possible that Jackson could handle Martin Beard.

"Is Jackson in his warehouse, Algur?"

"No."

"Get him," Fox commanded, and suddenly Jackson, back to his normal perfect self in spite of the wine, stood in front of Fox's desk, immaculate.

"Yes?"

"There is an old drunk at the Sifford town house, Jackson. He thinks he's Charles Sifford, old Charles Sifford, Mrs. Sifford's husband. The old drunk got into the town house, and the guard beat him to a pulp. The guard isn't supposed to do that. He's either supposed to shoot them dead, so they can't sue us, or at the least not leave a mark. This old man is a nut, Jackson, and kind of a law nut in a way. He's on the lookout for lawyers. So would you run over there and take him to an emergency room, in a taxi, and in general make sure he gets cleaned up.''

Was that all, Fox wondered, am I really thinking things through?

"I'm sorry to give you a stupid job like this," Fox added.

Jackson said nothing, but he looked a little sorry, too.

"At least you'll get to meet a girl named Fluffy. She's fun."

"Fine," Jackson said, and turned to go.

"Jackson, one more thing. Find out how he got in. They keep all the doors locked at the house. How did he get in?"

Jackson nodded, and turned again.

"Jackson," Fox said, "remember that. Please."

Jackson looked reproachful. Hadn't Fox learned by now? The last time Jackson had forgotten something was his lunch, once, in kindergarten.

"Algur," Fox shouted through his open door, "call reception and send whoever it is out there in."

Which she did.

28

THEY WERE IN the conversation pit. It was not where Fox wanted to be. He wanted to be in the erotic bed. Unfortunately, Kim Hartman, as usual, wanted to talk.

"How did he get into the house?"

"He had a key," Fox said.

"Oh, God," she said. "A key? How did he get a key?"

"Jackson will find that out," Fox said. "He's in the warehouse, running down Martin Beard's name."

"What does that mean?"

"He probably worked for the Siffords some time or other," Fox said. "So his name will be on some form or some check, and Jackson will find it. Simple."

"How many other weird, drunk bums have keys?" Kim Hartman asked.

"Who knows?"

Fox made a mental note to have the locks changed. Unfortunately, he was in no condition to be making mental notes: Kim Hartman distracted him.

"If he had a key," Kim said, "why did he come now? Why not right at the beginning?"

"Apparently Martin got drunk, really drunk, when he couldn't get a lawyer who would sue me."

"Sue you?"

"Sue the estate. He was Charles Sifford. He was going to sue the estate and break the will and get his money."

"He was more than drunk," she said. "They ought to lock him up."

"They have. The hospital has. Right now, he's got D.T.'s. And they'll give him dentures."

"Wonderful," Kim Hartman said.

How was he going to get her into the bedroom? The hell with Charles Sifford/Martin Beard. Or why not right here? Conversation pit? Love pit.

"No," Kim Hartman said. But at least she took hold of Fox's head and put it in her lap. He was lying on his back, his head in her lap, and looking up at her. She looked wonderful. And she was wearing his pearls.

"Talk to me," she said. "I do all the talking. You only ask questions."

Kim Hartman was expecting a lot from Fox. He had been trained to ask questions and not to talk.

He reached for her.

"No," she said. "Talk to me. It's much more important."

"Why?"

"Because I've been giving you a great deal of thought."

"Positive or negative?" Fox asked.

"Don't joke. Talk. I'm not kidding, Fox. You never talk about yourself. Is that because I don't let you? What would happen if we got married? I'd just sit and talk to you? Can I marry a man like that?"

I hope so, Fox thought. What am I suppose to talk

about? My day? Does she want to hear about taxes and old ladies, bank accounts and law briefs?

"All right," she said, "talk about your father. I see I've got to get you started. You're completely out of practice. How do you feel about your father."

How did he feel? A sudden smashing throbbing hit him in the forehead. As if a brick had fallen on his face. Why can't we engage in some form of nonverbal communication? he thought. But this was Kim Hartman, and if talk was what she wanted, Fox would try to forge ahead.

"Well," he said very slowly, "you know he's dead. He was a lawyer too." Fox stopped. He looked up at Kim Hartman. She understood.

"I can see that talking about your father is too difficult for you. All right then. Let's talk about why you got kicked out of school."

"How did you know about that?" Fox asked.

"You told me," she said, "in one of your rare unzipped moments."

"Zipped?"

"Another expression for 'wrapped tight.' I am picking up things from Fluffy."

"Fluffy is quite a girl," Fox said. "I wonder about how she got on with Jackson."

"Don't change the subject," Kim said. "Talk. Why didn't you grow up to be a preppie like your dad?"

"I *must* not have been wrapped tight," Fox said. "I told you that?"

"I think I extracted it from you with tweezers. I don't know. Now let's get talking. I'm leading up to trying to understand how you could have arrived at this fixation of yours on an older woman with a seventeen-year-old child. Let's hear about school, Fox. That's an easy question to get you going.''

Kim Hartman was on target. In her strange, unzipped way, she usually was. Why *did* Fox want to marry a forty-year-old woman with a teenage son? Why was it an obsession? There was a reason. The only problem was that Fox himself didn't know what the reason was. And tweezers were not enough to get the reason out of him.

He shut his eyes. She had her hand in his hair and that felt very good.

''I was kicked out because of the lunch line,'' he said. ''This was an all-boys' school of course, and we were supposed to line up for lunch. It's all very simple. I got in line. Then some big thug jumps me and tells me he is an upperclassman and the little weenies like me are supposed to go to the end of the line. All these people kept butting in ahead of me, and ordering me back. The same was true of all of us weenies. And these upperclassmen were big. I remember that they used to have pictures from *Playboy* taped inside their lockers. That was supposed to be very neat. Anyway, they all reminded me of my father, so I eventually slugged one.''

''A big thug?''

''A big thug,'' Fox said. ''And then eight of his friends threw me through a plate-glass window, and everyone said I had slipped. Even the little weenies. What did I expect? To lead a revolution? They were scared too. You understand, I was in the infirmary. This was some school. You pay I don't know how many thousand dollars a year to get your kid thrown through a window. Anyway, I kept punching, and they kept beating me up. What was the school going to do? Throw out the entire upper class? It was far simpler to eliminate me.''

''Was your dad angry?''

''My dad believed what the school told him. That I was a troublemaker.''

''Some father,'' Kim Hartman said.

The throbbing came back, and instinctively Kim Hartman softly rubbed Fox's forehead. He began to feel better again.

''He had his good points.''

''Like what?''

''He wrote very good letters. He fired them off to me almost every day I was in college, telling me exactly what to do and how to behave. That, of course, was because I had not gone to his school and obviously did not know how to deport myself. I ought to publish them sometime.''

''So you hated college?'' Kim Hartman said.

''Jesus,'' Fox said, ''haven't I talked enough?''

If we don't make love after this, I'm going to kill her, he thought. Why do I want to marry a forty-year-old woman? To make love with her. Is that hard to understand? He opened his eyes just enough so that he could see her shaking her head, the pearls shaking too, then closed them again.

''All right,'' he said, ''I had a wonderful time in college. All the thugs who had gone to the right school were trying to drink themselves to death, and catch girls, which they had been deprived of in the masochistic monastery, but this boy just wanted to learn how to write a paper. You know what I mean? I had come to college with the idea of being a star and famous, of course, but it did not take long for this boy to set his sights on a lesser attainment, which was to write a paper that might earn better than a C minus."

"Now you're talking," Kim Hartman said. "Good."

"Why do you sound so much like a shrink?" Fox asked.

"Because I was in analysis for eight years. Keep going."

Actually, Fox *was* beginning to talk, because this college thing brought back all kinds of strange feelings—of exertion, disgust, and, finally, triumph.

"It was like I wanted to get from Cambridge to Boston," Fox said, "but I didn't have a road map and hadn't heard about the subway, and got lost every time. Every time: C minus. There was some trick to writing a paper that wasn't a C minus, but I couldn't find it. I tried writing fancy and got an F. I tried writing abstractly and got a D. But basically, my whole life was a C minus. This was what I was worrying about while everyone else in my dorm was trying to drink himself to death. I remember driving up to Cape Cod, to my grandmother's summer house, with a friend . . ."

"A friend? I'll bet," Kim Hartman said.

"This friend always got an A and was a certified star who acted in plays at the Loeb Drama Center. We went up to the freezing Cape, in the dead of winter, and stayed in this drafty, huge old house, and I took the draft of a history paper and cut each individual sentence out, so that the paper lay all over a huge oak table in tiny little strips. I took the lamps from the living room and set them around the table. We had to wear our coats inside. The wind came in off the Sound, which was always white from the strong wind, and went right on into the house.

"Each of my sentences was a simple, declarative statement of fact. There were no transitions and no conclusions. To try to learn the trick, I'd boiled everything down to the basic elements. I remember exactly how it felt to walk around that big . . ."

Kim Hartman was doing something while he talked. He felt her hand move off his forehead, and then it came back, but he was rolling now, and didn't stop.

". . . table, blowing on my hands, and how I began to tape the little white strips to the table, leaving spaces between them for later additions. Fact following fact. Little strip of sentence following little strip, the big table turning white. I thought: This paper is going to be as solid as oak. I kept rearranging, reordering, taping, writing in little things, and then I had paragraph following paragraph, and finally the conclusion, the final fact that summarized all the other facts and was supported exactly by what had come before. This took me three days. I'm talking about a ten-page paper. On the third day, I added transitional sentences, and the paper was finished. I wonder about that girl. What did she think? Freezing for three days beside a maniac who cut his paper into small pieces and taped it to a table. What did she see in me? Then I put the typewriter down on the table, and started to type the paper in *final* draft form, moving all around the table, you see, as I followed my paper, line by line. That was college. It was fun. Cambridge is a strange place: all the students want to be stars. They join all sorts of clubs and become stars that are written up in the *Harvard Crimson*. There are political stars and literary stars, and movie stars too, now. Even the professors are stars. Galbraith was a star. Everyone wanted to be a star, but this boy, me, just wanted to write a paper that did not receive the grade of C minus. I wanted an A. Anyway, doing my papers that way, taping them to the table, starting with the basic elements, I learned the trick. After I learned the trick, I never wrote a paper that wasn't an A. I was a wonk, and very proud of myself.''

''What is a wonk?''

''A wonk is a person who is looked down upon because he gets very good grades and gets to go on to Harvard Law School, not the University of Virginia, and doesn't spend his entire college life drinking or trying to be a star that gets written about in the *Harvard Crimson*. That is a wonk. At least that is what they called them when I was in Cambridge.''

''You've been a good little wonk,'' Kim said. ''You've talked very well. You get an A.''

''Do I get to marry you?''

''I don't know, Fox,'' she said. She had stopped rubbing his head, and he opened his eyes.

She had taken off her pearls. Fox's mind clicked so fast and hard, it was almost as if he heard it make an actual sound. The old Southern saying...

''Yes, Fox,'' Kim said.

Once again she seemed to have read his mind.

29

Fox HAD WOKEN early, lying beside Kim, but she had refused to budge. He had kissed her to say good-bye, and her reaction had been to pull the pillow over her head and groan. So he had slipped out alone, to get to his own apartment, shower, dress in a clean suit, and then he would go to the office early. And Jackson would be there. It did not seem to matter how early Fox arrived. Jackson seemed to anticipate his moves by extrasensory perception. This guy will make president, Fox thought. I come in at five-thirty in the morning, and somehow he knows I'm going to do it and beats me to the office. Jesus, they turn out robots now from the Harvard Law School, all equipped with sensors. Preprogrammed to please and do everything just right, but inhuman. And then he reminded himself that Jackson indeed had proved to be human, and that he, Fox, had promised not to give Jackson any more trouble. With Jackson anyway the robotization hadn't gone right. The robot planners had forgotten to give him a stomach.

Jackson *was* there, before even Fox's secretary had arrived. Fox said hello, politely, and told Jackson to sit down. If he didn't tell Jackson to sit down,

Jackson would stand. It's not *all* my fault, Fox thought, he does some of it to himself.

"I thought you would like to know that I have confirmed that Mr. Beard worked for the Siffords," Jackson said. "According to the warehouse files, he left at the time Mr. Sifford left. And I think you would be interested in knowing that Mr. Sifford's account paid his salary."

"What did he do?" Fox asked.

"I've got no idea," Jackson said. "I suppose he was some sort of flunky." Jackson glared at Fox.

Flunky? Fox thought. What is Jackson talking about? If anything, Martin Beard, the lunatic, was some sort of valet to Mr. Sifford. And one who probably drank with Mr. Sifford, sneaking, preparing, and sharing Bloody Marys that the Virgin Mary, Mrs. Sifford, would not allow. Probably he had also arranged meetings between Mr. Sifford and Mrs. Banning.

"I thought you would be interested in one further piece of information." Now Jackson actually smiled. It was the first time Fox had ever seen his smile, and Fox was astonished. "I thought you would be interested in knowing Mr. Beard's present employer."

Jackson seemed to realize he was smiling, and immediately stopped. For God's sake, Fox thought, don't be embarrassed about smiling. But Fox didn't say that, though he almost did. One little gold school star for me, Fox thought.

"His present employer is Mr. Marsiglia."

"How the hell did you find that out?"

"I took him to the emergency room," Jackson said slowly. "They don't let you in there until they've got your Blue Cross card, and all the rest of it. It was all there in his wallet, and I had to help get the stuff out.''

''What does he do for Marsiglia,'' Fox said. ''Drink?''

''I don't know. I couldn't ask him. First of all, he was pretty messed up and had no teeth to speak of. Second, he was drunk out of his skull. And third, the man is a lunatic.''

''You did a good job on this, Jackson,'' Fox said. ''Thanks.''

''Of course I did a good job. I've had some experience with emergency rooms. I suppose that's why you picked on me for the job.''

Why does Jackson sound so suspicious? Fox wondered. Does he think I've got a lot of other secret horrible jobs I'm planning to send him on? It was, after all, only one trip to an emergency room. Oh well, Fox thought, Gauder always said that everyone turns suspicious when someone dies. You can't help that, Gauder said, because they're right to be suspicious. Another death is always right around the corner.

''By the way, the police were at the hospital.''

''What!'' Fox said.

Fox had been through a lot of messy estates, and funny divorce actions, and times when people had threatened to kill each other: rich young couples had stood on each side of his desk screaming at each other and threatening each other, and once, a young girl who was trying to give fifteen million to the Moonies but was unable to because of the way Fox had drafted her trust fund had gone right out on his window ledge and threatened to jump. And Fox had seen embezzlement and stock manipulation and suicide. But he had never once had the police involved in anything; that was not, as Gauder had once said, the way things were done.

"What did *they* want?"

"You couldn't exactly say he'd tripped and fallen. The guy was a complete mess. Beard looked like he'd been run over. Your guard really killed him."

My guard? Fox wondered. My guard *killed* him? It was obvious that Jackson did not understand the rules: nobody kills anybody. And then Fox wondered: How well does Marsiglia understand the rules? I've got to keep Jackson on a leash, Fox thought. He's a very strange young man, and he makes me nervous.

"The guard's been bored with nothing to do. Remind me to change him. And complain to the damn security company."

Jackson's eyes clicked: With Jackson, Fox thought, you don't ever have to make notes. He just clicked everything into his data bank.

"So I told them, the police, the truth. And they wanted to arrest him."

"The guard?" Fox said, not thinking.

"Beard, for robbery. They don't care about the guard. He used to be a police officer himself."

"You stopped them, I hope."

"No," Jackson said slowly. "I didn't."

"What?"

"I couldn't reach you. Look, all of this took some time. I tried you at the firm. I tried you at your apartment. No luck. So I decided to act on my own initiative. I figured wherever you were, you did not want to be disturbed. If you know what I mean."

Fox knew, because there was a peculiar idiot grin on Jackson's face: he knew Fox had been with Kim Hartman. How did Jackson find that out? Fox wondered.

"All right, Jackson," Fox said. "Look, just give me some facts, please. You say you acted on your own initiative. Just what sort of initiative did you initiate?"

"I called Marsiglia," Jackson said.

"You what?" Fox exploded, and stood up. "You got through to Marsiglia?"

"Did you want the guy arrested and put in jail and then something in the newspapers? No, you didn't. Now here is what I thought is interesting. And, if I may say so, is exactly what I predicted would happen. Within five minutes, the police get the message, and there aren't going to be any charges. What do you think of that?"

"And just what the hell did Marsiglia say when you called him?"

"'Thank you,'" Jackson said, and for the second time in his relationship with Fox, he smiled.

30

FOX GAVE JACKSON an assignment: to go back to the hospital and get Martin Beard to sign a release form that stated that Beard would not sue the estate for the beating, in return for which the estate would not sue Beard for trespass. Fox added, "While you're there, Jackson, see if you can get some useful information out of your lunatic." Then Fox turned to his window to meditate. He didn't get much time.

"A Mr. Sneed is on the line," Miss Algur said from the door. Sneed? Fox gradually heard Algur, put it together, and picked up his phone.

"Foxy, you want to have lunch with me?"

It was the last thing Fox wanted. One lunch with Sneed had been plenty.

"Why?"

"Because I have information you need. So meet me at my club."

"Just where is your club?"

"Midtown, One eighty East Seventieth, on the thirtieth floor. Got that? And one more thing, Foxy, will you take a cab? I'll even pay for it."

Fox marched up Wall Street with the crowd, looking for a cab, and met a mumbler. There were so many people pouring out of the big buildings that the mumbler blocked the flow. Everyone had to move around him. He was like a jagged boulder popping up unexpectedly and breaking the flow of a small, calm stream. Fox had gotten himself into the flow of traffic that moved right past the mumbler himself, and it made Fox nervous: the man was wearing a gray loose coat like a messenger's. He stood in the middle of Wall Street, one foot planted in front of him, his eyes glazed. He was punching out at the air, as if there were some invisible boxer in front of him, and he was yelling, with every punch: "That's yours, take it, take it, that's yours."

Sometimes, Fox thought, the mumblers scream about their wife, sometimes it's their father. He wondered what particular demon had decided to strike this mumbler today. This one is a borderline mumbler, Fox thought, about to turn into a certified maniac who might hurt people. I don't like those punches. And usually they walk as they mumble, he thought. This time, the police will probably take him away. Punch: a scream, and Fox, with his briefcase up as a shield, managed to get by, get lucky, and find a cab.

Yes, Fox thought, cursing Sneed now, I take a cab and what do I get? The man seemed to drive at about ten miles an hour. He carefully avoided every pothole. There are so many potholes in New York City that the cab constantly swerved in a crazy slow-motion pattern that was like an instant replay, also in slo-mo, of some hot-dog skier. There was also the problem of how they would get from Wall Street to Rockefeller Center. The man was taking a route that

147

involved streets even Fox had never seen. Apparently, he's found the streets with the least potholes, Fox thought, giving the driver the benefit of the doubt, and not wondering whether the guy was just trying to jack up the fare.

It's going to take almost an hour to get to Rockefeller Center, Fox thought. It would have taken eight minutes in the subway. In fact the taxi driver was ingenious: he had gotten Fox to Midtown in less than fifteen minutes. Fox hadn't bothered to look at his watch.

The fare was substantial, and Fox pulled out a twenty-dollar bill, which was all he had.

"Hey, I don't have change for a twenty," the cab driver said.

Suddenly, it was too much for Fox. "What do you plan to do," he said. "Drive to a bank and get some, and charge me for that too?"

"Listen, wise guy," the driver said. "Listen, nut."

"Now, your bank is probably in Brooklyn, right?" Fox said. "And you live there too, so we'll stop for lunch, while you go to get the change." Fox was rolling: the beautiful day was turning bad fast. "And it will take you so long to drive to your bank that I'll probably have to baby-sit your repulsive children."

"You just give me your twenty, and sit in the cab and wait, understand buddy. I'll get your change. You comprendo?"

"I comprendo," Fox said. "You're a cab driver; I'm a lawyer. I'm in the business of writing papers and signing them, so I carry a pen. You're in the business of cab driving. Comprendo? So you're supposed to have change in the cab. You're supposed to make change. Well, make it. Or no fare."

It was a beautiful cab, but it didn't have one of those bulletproof Plexiglas partitions between the front and the rear. The cab driver turned around, ripped the twenty out of Fox's hand, and locked Fox in the cab. He was a very good driver, and not stupid. He even took the car keys. Like most city cabs, the cab was designed so that the passenger can't get out until he pays. Fox sat fuming for what he perceived to be a full twenty minutes, before the driver opened the back door, and threw Fox's change down on the sidewalk.

"And I took out a tip too," the cab driver yelled. "And a big one, Mr. Suit."

Suit? Fox thought, Mr. Suit? Did all of this happen just because I wear suits? He gave up on the day and began picking up his change, humbly, thinking: I look like one of those poor slobs who goes down Fifth Avenue, looking into all the garbage cans and picking out the good stuff. The only difference is that I wear a suit. I am a recalcitrant bum. What's wrong with me? Why am I now yelling at cab drivers? Why am I turning rude? *Why am I horrible?*

Sneed's club was one of the newest in New York, and probably the darkest, Fox thought. It was definitely a fast boy club. There was a lot of steel and recessed lighting, and something about it vaguely reminded Fox of Kim's apartment, in which the designer had tried to communicate about sex. Midtown is really where the fast boys live, Fox thought. In the shiny new office buildings are the venture capital firms, with names like Emerald Fund and Gonad Corp., and you never exactly really know where all their money comes from.

Well, actually, some of it, a lot of it, came from the Midwest. Fox knew that. Funny, Fox thought, if you read the papers you'd believe that it's all Arab money or European money, but a lot of it, maybe most of it, is from the Midwest. The Midwest is a huge place, he thought. And in each of its hundreds of cities there is usually one family or maybe two who have made a killing, slowly, over several generations and own the bank and a farm or two. They have perhaps sixty million dollars, and some of the sixty goes to the solid banks, like Morgan, but a little extra million or so on the side goes to the venture capital firms, at high risk, and fast boys take it and promise to deliver returns in the nature of two thousand percent, if you strike it. You might not, but if you did strike it, you might turn into a Carnegie or a Mellon, or some damn thing.

And all your children would move to New York, Fox thought. The money goes to the venture capital boys and their little companies, and they go around searching for very, very smart wonks who have invented something like the Xerox machine or the computer, and are regarded as lunatics by everyone in the neighborhood, because they are always down there in the cellar tinkering with their contraptions.

Sometimes, they did find a very, very smart wonk, and they gave him the money to make a prototype of his invention and in return took fifty percent of the company. Then everyone got very, very rich. Of course, the smart wonk who had, say, invented the airplane should have gotten a lot richer than he did. He never should have signed over fifty percent of his company, but there was so much money nobody complained very much.

Around the tables in the dark room of Sneed's club Fox saw earnest young men leaning forward, their heads in the shadows, whispering. Why whisper? he wondered. The place had carpeting on the walls. You could barely hear anyone anyway. Fox's own club, which was on Wall Street, was very old, and going bankrupt, and the rugs were threadbare. It let in almost anybody. Even people like Fox who had been kicked out of prep school and had no real connections and were just ordinary partners, in ordinary old-time law firms. But it had quite a reputation. He belonged to that club because Gauder had insisted on it.

"You look distracted," Sneed said. "Flaked."

"I was concentrating on details, when I should have allowed my mind to float."

"What does that mean?" Sneed said.

"Nothing," Fox said.

He had been trying to understand why he'd yelled at the cab driver. Why his mind had gotten busted up. That happened to you in New York. It was too much of a town.

"Snap out of it," Sneed said. "I have. Tomorrow I'm going to Singapore."

"Why?"

"Does it matter?" Sneed said. "Just a deal. But the adrenaline is building. Maybe I'll keep going into big new open China and sell them Japan. You're wondering why I wanted to have lunch with you?"

"You're right." But actually Fox wasn't wondering. He was thinking this: There's some *meaning* in the way I reacted to that cab driver and that mumbler, some damn sea change in my mind. *What?*

"Have you ever done anything wrong?" Sneed said. "Something like a little old embezzlement, or perhaps a little cheating on your income tax? Ever, say, overbilled a client or murdered an old lady?"

Fox was clean as a whistle. He didn't bother to answer.

"Because if you have, it's coming back to haunt you."

"How?"

"Someone wants to know."

Now, like everyone else in this dark club, Fox hunched forward and leaned toward Sneed: "Do I have to play games with you again? Just like when we were associates and shared an office, and you made everything a game? What is happening?"

Sneed nodded his head. "Did I give you a lot of trouble back then?" he asked, and seemed genuinely concerned.

"Sneed," Fox said, "I like you, but you always made me feel insecure. As if you were going to make partner and I wasn't. I wasn't all that sorry to see you go. Do you remember any of that? You used to look me up and down and then tell me that some partner had telephoned me on days when I was late for work. Or you would remind me, in an elevator crowded with people, that my memorandum for some partner, say for Gauder, was three days late. So, truthfully, yes, you gave me trouble back then. And you played games. I'm just glad you found an area of the legal world in which you can channel your special kind of energy.''

"How is Gauder?" Sneed said.

"Almost gone."

"Was I really that bad?" Sneed said. "Christ."

"That bad," Fox said. "I won't even bother to remind you about the firm dance."

"Oh God," Sneed said. Then, he looked up at the dark ceiling, smiled, and added: "Oh well."

"So," Fox said, "no games. *Why are we having lunch?* What does this all mean?"

"What you just did is amazing," Sneed laughed. "What's happening to you, Fox? Last time you bought pearls. This time you actually reveal something of your true feelings to another human being. You know the entire time we shared that office, you said, good morning, good afternoon, good evening, and good night. That was it. You were impossible, too, and all I was just trying to do was goad you into being human."

"I'm tired, Sneed," Fox said. "I'm cranky, and I'm confused. What's happening? Please?"

"Marsiglia is checking you out. And he can do it. I thought you ought to know. It takes connections and money, and politics and other things, which you know all about, to build the huge projects he's doing now. Marsiglia is running you over very fine. He has the connections to do it. He's probably got all your tax forms by now, and your banking statements, and probably your report cards."

Fox flashed on the time he'd been kicked out of school, and for an instant, he thought, crazily: Yes, it does all come back to haunt you. I'll get thrown in jail because I was thrown out of school.

"How do you know all this?" Fox said.

"Extrapolation, Fox. Reasoning. And luck. We shared that office, remember? I have some friends. My own bank records were run through a computer. Why? Because I shared that office with you. I don't know, Fox. Marsiglia is combing you pretty fine. Why? Why bother? Marsiglia, by the way, is a member of this club, so if he shows up here for lunch, we can ask him."

"Great," said Fox in disgust.

"Listen," Sneed said, "I know you. You've never done anything wrong in your life."

So then Marsiglia will have to shoot me, Fox thought, or invent something I did wrong. Old Gauder taught me the rules, only now I'm not sure anyone else knows them. Fox wondered how much teaching Marsiglia had gotten from his father and the Siffords. What kind of education had he had?

"Well that's it," Sneed said. "I thought, hell, if Fox does have anything to hide, he ought to get cracking on it. Anything to hide?"

"You think I'd tell you?" Fox said. "Maybe you work for Marsiglia. You belong to his club. You probably voted him in."

"Well, he did build it," Sneed said, with a big smile, as if he had just played another trick on Fox, as if they were still young associates. "Tomorrow it's Singapore," Sneed added. "Let me know how it all turns out."

154

31

HE TOOK THE subway back to Wall Street. No more cabs for the time being. The subway ride went pretty well. He stared at the advertisements and ignored the general filth and drunk teenagers. It was a compromise.

Normally, Fox would have rolled up his newspaper to zap some mugger in the stomach if an attack came. Now he threw his brain into remote control, radar takeover, and relied on his years riding this subway. All these years of care had implanted a sort of Spider-Man tingling-sense telepathy, so that he actually now believed that he could feel a mugger coming, even if he was concentrating on the ad for Grant's Scotch. Which is what I need right now, Fox thought, a big bottleful. And some cash.

Fox's bank was "full service," and since Fox was a partner in the law firm that used it, he had been assigned a smart, pretty young "junior officer." For some reason, women, who had always been tellers, were now the loan officers and the junior executives, and all of them were climbing the banking hierarchy fast.

It didn't all have to do with the ERA. It had to do with the changing image of the banks: "macho banking," "the fast banker," "the sexy banker." Fox had even seen an honest-to-God ad in the *New York Times* magazine section which showed a beautiful young girl being stared at by some young fast boy who was supposedly admiring her clothes, not her fantastic body. The copy read: "So you're a loan officer. I thought you were a model."

Fox's "personal banker" could have been a model too. She had blonde hair and blue eyes that seemed to stretch around to her ears. Fox sat down, and wrote out a check for three hundred dollars. A messenger emerged behind her and took the check from her hand.

"How are you today, Mr. Fox?" He told her he was great, and asked how much money he had in his checking account.

"Seven thousand two hundred and twenty dollars. I think we ought to move some of that into your custodial account and zap some T bills."

She had not picked up the phone. She just knew how much money was in his account. How? Did Marsiglia own his bank, or build it? And call up his personal banker and tell her to send over all the files?

In fact, the girl knew how much money was in Fox's account because she daydreamed that Fox would ask her out for lunch. But Fox had enough trouble trying to understand Kim Hartman. How could he be expected to read the secret messages that the fast girls send as they communicate their attraction and ask for a response?

The woman at the bank had made Fox think of Marsiglia. And Fox was still thinking of Marsiglia as he walked home in the dark from the subway, down the row of apartment houses toward his own. Where Marsiglia owned the buildings, the doormen were dressed like the male flight attendants on TWA: they had black double-breasted coats and military type hats with silver braid.

Fox had, before, always thought it quite a uniform—much better than the frilly circus stuff they wore on the other airlines—but now, passing Marsiglia's buildings on his way home, his brains scrambled by a tough day and his lunch with Sneed, he saw each of the doormen as a foreign agent, watched their eyes, thinking that at any time, one might leap out at him, grab him around the neck, strangle him, and blame it on some mugger. Think straight, Fox told himself, but he couldn't.

His own building was not owned by Marsiglia, and his own doorman was lying on the fancy couch beside the glass front door. Fox had to pound for a long time before he got in, and finally up to his apartment. There, leaning against the door was a box. A bomb, he thought. Then: No, think straight, it's a present from Kim Hartman. And he forgot the day for a second, took the box into his kitchen, and ripped it open.

Oranges. Big fat perfect orange-colored oranges from Oregon, with a big note from Lou and Bill who ran "the best fruit farm in the state," and wanted to tell Fox all about it in the enclosed brochure, which would also explain exactly what fruit he would be getting each month for the next twelve months as a member of the Fruits Unlimited Club, and how to eat and serve it—all of this thanks to his benefactress,

Kimberly Hartman. Her name was spelled out in big gold letters.

Instructions to eat oranges? Fox wondered. Do they include that with every order? Or does that only go to New York, where Lou and Bill probably think everyone goes out to restaurants all the time and no one knows how to peel.

Well, it is at least an interesting present, he thought. You give pearls. You get oranges. He was eating one of them in the telephone room, peeled without reference to the instructions of Lou and Bill, and was at the same time dialing the number of Kim Hartman.

She didn't answer. Instead, Fox got some clown with a fake British accent, which Fox instantly recognized as the kind of accent that is mandatory at Sotheby Parke Bernet, or at a gallery. A twit accent. They favor dark suits. Fox asked the twit if Mrs. Hartman was at home. Yes, she most certainly was, Fox was told, and then Fox was asked if he thought he might be able to hold the "tele" for a few seconds or so. It turned out that he had to hold the "tele" for a good long time. By the time Kim picked up the phone, Fox had already run through an entire scenario in which she was lying in bed with a fake British twit who had been told to muzzle his laughter by putting a pillow over his face.

"What the hell was that?" Fox said.

"A friend," Kim Hartman told him. "Listen, it's all too complicated to explain right now, and I'm incredibly busy."

I'll bet, Fox thought. Christ Jesus.

"Is it important, Fox?" she said. "Or can it wait?"

Wait for what, his mind went spinning, until you finish?

"Fox," Kim said. "Why did you call?"

"The oranges," he said feebly.

"Yes," she said. "They are special ones from a hothouse in Oregon. You need to keep your health up. You work too hard. And you get colds all the time. This will load you up with vitamin C. And I want you to start exercising too. We'll talk about that, later. Is there anything else?"

"Could we see each other?" he said, his voice barely audible. He *could* hear a sort of rustling in the background, which sounded exactly like one sheet being pulled over another. It *was* material of some sort. Maybe the man was getting undressed. Oh no, no, he thought, please no.

"Of course," Kim said.

"Now? Or a little later in the evening?" Fox suggested.

"Not now," Kim answered. "Listen, I've got to get on with this. I just can't talk. Call me tomorrow."

Get on with it? he thought, and for the second time that day, Fox became emotionally labile in a way that was uncharacteristic. He yelled into the old black telephone: "I know you could come and see me if you wanted to. You could dump that twit English butler down the elevator shaft, if you wanted to, that asshole who answered your phone, and probably got his accent from studying a British Airways commercial. You could get rid of him all right, you just don't feel like it, what you feel like is one great big..."

She hung up. He set down the phone. Scotch, he thought, like a dying man crossing the Sahara who

spies a demitasse of water in the distance. *Scotch.*
There was just enough for one huge glass. Then the
cupboard was bare. He would have to drink cognac.
That would mean a huge headache in the morning.
He drank the Scotch, then switched to cognac, and
slowly began to calm, and fell onto the sofa drunk, to
watch his antique wooden black and white television
with its small round screen.

The old round eye seemed to be giving Fox crazy
messages. All the actresses looked like Kim Hartman.
All the men looked like Marsiglia. Then the program
he had been watching turned into a talk show, and he
was watching television celebrities. And in a very
drunk way, thinking: Where is my rock? Where is my
anchor? What is the state of the world? What clubs
do the new celebrities belong to? They belong to
some club, too. It is all getting mixed up, the passing
of money, how much do the new celebrities make,
you make enough, and it gets passed along, everything has changed since Gauder was young and, like
the flickering eye of his old television, you could not
hold the image right, it moved too fast for this drunk
man, for me, Fox thought, no anchor, Kim Hartman,
Marsiglia, money, Kim...

32

IN THE MORNING, Fox got his headache, got it good, and in general did not look very well. He had expected that he would see the impeccable Jackson first thing and that Jackson's impeccability, contrasted with Fox's wasted washed-out looks, would make him, Fox, feel his usual anger. And therefore, because of Jackson's stomach, Fox took a triple vow not to be rude. In fact, Jackson looked worse than Fox. His eyes were huge black circles. He swayed slightly in front of Fox's desk.

"Jackson," Fox said, "please sit down."

Jackson fell into a chair.

"What is it!" Fox said. "The stomach? Is it a delayed reaction to that wine? Listen, you don't have to come into work every day. Not if you're sick. Are you sick?"

"No," Jackson said.

"Listen, is it something personal, something wrong with your family. Did your mother die or something?"

That remark was something that even Fox realized was a drastic mistake. What if his mother has died? Fox suddenly thought. What's wrong with me? Then: oh well, Jackson will probably roll over clutching his stomach. What can I do about it? There is never a day off for a future president. Jackson's mother has died, and he's come to work anyway.

"No," Jackson said slowly, "everything is fine with my family."

"Well, something is the matter."

"A personal matter."

"You're not going to tell me?"

"Sir, I have a lot to tell you," Jackson said. "First, I could not get Martin Beard to sign the release form."

"What's the problem?" Fox said. "He has a lawyer already? Some ambulance chaser got to him?"

"He never got a chance to sign our release form, because he wasn't there," Jackson said.

"I thought they had him locked up in some special detoxification unit reserved for complete nuts."

"They did," Jackson groaned, "but Marsiglia got him out. And took him somewhere, I guess. I would guess probably took him to the East River and put him down on the bottom."

"Come on, Jackson."

"Anyway, he's gone."

"How could Marsiglia get him out?"

"How would I know," Jackson growled. His head must be hurting him more than mine hurts me, Fox thought. What has happened to Jackson? What happened to Martin Beard? Who the hell was with Kim Hartman last night? Stick with Martin Beard, Fox concluded.

"I don't know," Jackson went on. "Listen, maybe

Marsiglia offered to endow a special unit for the hospital. I mean, Beard apparently signed out against doctor's orders and all kinds of other restraints. Plus there is an ordinance that requires lunatics to be institutionalized and evaluated, which the hospital apparently ignored. So maybe Marsiglia also offered to pick up the tab if Martin Beard now goes out and murders someone, whose family then sues the hospital for negligence. I don't know how Marsiglia got him out. I just know he did.''

"How do you know?''

"Who else could?'' Jackson groaned. "I didn't see any special form. Marsiglia didn't leave a note. But who else would care about a lunatic drunk who doesn't know how to do anything but make trouble. And besides, who else knew Beard was in the hospital? Anyway, I see it as a perfect solution to one problem.''

"What problem?''

"You can bet Beard isn't going to sue the estate, or anyone else for that matter. You can bet Marsiglia is going to make sure he doesn't walk around mumbling anymore. He must have something to mumble about, which is why Marsiglia hired him, and now will kill him.''

"Do not talk about people getting killed,'' Fox snapped.

"They do, don't they,'' Jackson said. "Partners in Wall Street law firms off each other. There's the case of...''

Fox's own head now hurt too much to run through that case. It was a special case, anyway, where a former attorney general of the United States, and a senior partner, had shot the head of the corporate department over adultery.

"We do not talk about that one, Jackson," Fox growled. "We don't even think about it. You joined a stodgy firm. We don't off anyone here. Stop talking about murder."

Jackson shook his head. As if he wanted to make sure it was still in existence and had not fried itself in pain.

"Could I ask a personal favor?" he said slowly. Jackson doesn't want to say it, Fox thought. You can hear the pain in his voice. Jackson wanted to be perfect, and for once in his life, he wasn't. He wanted to keep going, but he couldn't. Fox smiled, and Jackson caught it.

"Forget it," Jackson said.

"Please," Fox said, "please go ahead."

Jackson's in precarious balance, Fox thought. I've got to find out what's going on with him.

"All right," Jackson said. "If it would not unduly hinder the operations of the firm, I would like to request one day of vacation time. Today."

"You don't need a day of vacation," Fox said. "You don't even need sick leave. I will permit you to go home and sleep, and I won't tell a single soul about it. All right? If anyone asks, I'll tell them I've given you a secret assignment."

33

KIM HARTMAN called Fox at about four in the afternoon, and asked: "Have you returned to normality?"

"Yes," Fox lied.

Of course he had not returned to anything close to normality. But it helped him a lot to be talking to Kim Hartman again, instead of fighting with her.

"Then I thought I'd invite myself over to your place and spend the night."

My place, Fox wondered, why my place?

There was a lot on Fox's mind. And he had trouble understanding what was happening. He had trouble knowing that something *was* happening. He really wanted to be at Kim Hartman's place. With Kim. The old relics in Fox's apartment disturbed him.

"Why can't we go to your place?"

"None of your business," she said. "Please give me an answer. Can I come?"

"Yes."

"Good," she answered. "Then I'm going to leave the abominable Sifford town house, and be there waiting for you. When do you expect to make it?"

He expected to make it right away. He told her

that, and got hung up on. Then he started to call for Jackson, forgetting that he'd sent Jackson home. There was a big fat pile of paper on Fox's desk, work that he had not done and should do. He stared at it, and thought about Kim Hartman, and then picked up the intercom, and got the associate lawyer who shared Jackson's office. Did the boy know anything about estates and trusts? Could he create a foreign trust and avoid United States taxation? Fox had no idea. But they were all quick learners, these fast boys, so Fox decided to give him a chance. He could learn all night.

It was twilight as Fox walked to his apartment, and the sky was purple and red. It was the time in this city that Fox liked best. Everyone was happy: because everyone was going home or out for the evening. And tonight, as well, there was a strong hot wind. Beautiful women dressed all up came out on the streets, their perfume snaking behind them, as they headed for meetings, and early dinners, and the theater. And, Fox thought, I've got a beautiful woman waiting for me.

She *was* waiting, making the dinner, on the practical grounds that Fox could not cook. Fox could make a peanut butter sandwich, a B.L.T, and French toast. That was it. And that was exactly what he made himself for dinner when he ate alone at his apartment, unless he ordered out. He was very good at ordering out, and sometimes, when he was feeling very sorry for himself, he ordered out from one of the fancy places, like Sandando, where they bring you a complete perfect French dinner, all neatly packaged in little frozen containers, with instructions as to how to assemble it. Fox could use his microwave oven and in this way have himself a fine dinner if he was alone and in a bad mood.

Craig Claiborne says that microwave ovens aren't any good. They aren't, unless you're a thirty-six-year-old lawyer fast on your way to endless bachelorhood. Then they're a necessity.

What Kim Hartman made were steaks, which she had brought herself, along with the wine. They got through dinner and did the dishes together. It was only after they'd had an after-dinner drink that he could control himself no longer and asked about the twit.

"Who was that friend of yours?" he said.

"What friend?"

"The English gentleman who answered your phone," Fox said, thinking, the stupid, fake, twit, rat *motherfucker.*

"English gentleman?" Kim said. She had this way of smiling, so that although she was forty, it sometimes made her look as if she were sixteen and just having a great time being exactly who she was and where she was, concentrating on the immediate moment. She gave Fox one of those smiles. And she reached out her long arm and held Fox's hand.

"I'm not having an affair with anyone," she said.

"No one-night stands?"

"Nothing," she said. "What's wrong with me?"

"Then who was the twit?"

"I'm not going to tell you," she said.

"You're just going to keep me in a state of continuous agitation?"

"Fox," she said, smiling, and looking right into his eyes, "I'm not having an affair. Do you think I'd lie to you?"

It was her smile, and partly the Sifford matter. The Sifford matter was making Fox believe that everyone was lying to him. Yes, he thought Kim Hartman might lie to him. Of course.

"You'd never lie, Kim," Fox said.

"Everything will come clear in the end, darling. Wait patiently. You must learn less agitation and try to learn to be calm. Which is exactly what I tell Fluffy."

Less agitation? Kim Hartman was agitated all the time. But Fox gave up on the twit. She was not going to tell him, and he did not want to fight with her, because he did not want to end up sleeping on the sofa in his own apartment.

"How is Fluffy?" he said.

Kim Hartman let go of Fox's hand and lit the one cigarette she allowed herself each day. Since she didn't inhale, Fox thought, this concept of cutting down was ridiculous.

"Fluffy is driving me crazy with her Southern accent, her Southern chic."

"Southern chic?" Fox said.

"It's the sign of the times, of my age, my generation. You see, now it is nineteen eighty, and now it is very fashionable to have a Southern accent. Do you understand what I mean?"

"Explain it to me," Fox said.

"When I grew up, it was not fashionable to talk Southern in a Northern college, and definitely not fashionable to talk Southern in this city. Which is why I do not have a Southern accent. And, yes, I hated my mother. But I got back at her. I drove her crazy when I came home cleansed of my Southern accent. She 'blessed me out.'"

"She what?" Fox asked.

"You don't curse, Fox. I'm talking Southern now. What you do is bless people out. What it means is to tell them to go to hell."

"You've been through a lot," Fox said.

"Not me," she said, "I'm beginning to think you've been through more than I have. The only difference is that you won't talk about it. You want to talk about Fluffy. All right, Fox. The point of it is that now having a Southern accent is very fashionable. Do you think Fluffy's stupid?"

"I wondered how she got through Radcliffe talking the way she does."

"They loved her at Radcliffe. They love her in New York. Fluffy talks more Southern here in New York than she does in Charleston. Fluffy talks Daddy. 'Mah daddy se-as this. Mah daddy se-as that.' Fluffy se-as 'Mistah Fox looks just like mah daddy.'"

"Oh Jesus," Fox said.

"What's the matter?"

"Am I that old?"

"She has ah very young daddy, Mistah Fox."

"Marry me," Fox said, "or there's no hope."

"That matter is under consideration," Kim Hartman said as she snuffed out what was left of the cigarette and stood up. "Let's go for it," she said.

"Go for it?"

"It's a Southern expression, a kind of cross between an exclamation of achievement and a com-

169

mand to do something. Go for it. In this particular situation, the phrase means about the same thing as taking off my pearls.''

34

THEY WENT FOR it, but not until Kim Hartman had changed the sheets. She did it very slowly, making precise hospital corners. Goddamn my cleaning lady, how could she forget the bed? Fox thought as he watched Kim, his desire to grab her rising with his anger. Damn the cleaning lady: everything is breaking down, the cleaning lady, Jackson, the whole city. He had tried to help Kim, but she said no. Fox could not cook, but he could make a bed. He could make one very, very fast if it was going to have Kim Hartman in it. But Kim made the bed excruciatingly slowly, and by the time they went for it, Fox was more than ready, and it all went very, very fast.

Afterward, lying there in the dark, he turned serious with her.

''You say getting married is under consideration.'' He was lying on his back and she was spread all over his chest. ''What goes into the equation?''

''You talk about 'just getting married,' '' she said. ''You've never been married. You won't understand.''

''Try me,'' he said.

"How would we get along?"

"Any way you want to."

"That's what you say now."

"It's what I'll say then," he said, and he meant it. He just really wanted to live with her.

"No you wouldn't. There are hundreds of little things, and big ones too, and you might want a child. Another child? I don't know, Fox."

"We'd hire someone to take care of the child."

"You think having children is like a law firm, where you just hire another associate? You see what I mean, Fox? There are hundreds of things we don't know about. Your mind is one."

"What other things?"

"I don't like being older than you."

"That doesn't matter," Fox said. What was four years?

"It matters to me. I can't explain it."

It must have mattered to her, because she rolled off his chest, and lay next to him, so they were no longer touching.

"There is my child."

"I like Robert."

"That's nice. Robert hates you," Kim said. "He hates everybody right now. It's a stage. The only person Robert likes is his father, who is a maniac."

"He hates me?" Fox said, thinking of all the presents he'd been sending Robert. Can't you buy off anybody anymore? Robert was a punk.

"But he is really already formed," Kim said. "I don't know. It doesn't matter what he thinks. There is my business. Would I have to give it up? I don't know, Fox. You'd want a child, and you say we'd

171

have help, but one does want to be with a child. So the business goes. You really don't understand. They understand now, though. Fluffy understands, I'm sure of that. She'll have it all plotted out. And it will work for her. But I got born at just the wrong time. Young enough to see it happen, but too old to really make my own choices. I didn't plot anything out. And look what the hell happened. Look who I married. And why? And having a child when I understood absolutely nothing about children? I actually thought: Yes, this is what you're supposed to do. Have a child. At twenty-three. I didn't plan anything out, and for that reason, nothing worked out, and this time I am really going to think it through."

"What does that mean?" Fox said.

"There are a lot of options. We might try living together on a regular basis. We might just keep going on the way we are."

"Or we might get married," Fox said.

"Why do *you* want to get married?" she asked. And came back to him, spreading herself over him again, and he put his arm around her.

"I guess I'd like to pin you down."

"You see what I mean: pin me down. It's your kind of mind. Pin her down, nail down the deal, sign the contract. And then forget about it. See?"

"You're wrong," he said.

"I just don't understand you, Fox. I know you moved into this apartment when your father died. But you haven't changed anything, anything at all. Like your little telephone room. It's very quaint. And so is your old round television. But why won't you buy a

172

new bed? This damn thing is pretty lumpy. Why don't you make some changes? Why, Fox?''

"I don't know. There hasn't been time.''

"There's been plenty of time. Two years. Why didn't your father modernize the place? For some reason, you want to hold on to this place, and keep it just the way it was in the forties. But at the same time, you're ready to give everything up for me. I just don't understand you. So how can I marry you?''

"I love you.''

"How can I tell?'' Kim asked, talking to herself. "Oh, Fox,'' she said finally, "I know I'm wrong. I know you love me.''

"You do?''

"I'm not an idiot,'' she said drowsily. "I can see quite clearly that you love me like mad and want me so much you can't stand it, and actually that is the only reason I've even taken the subject of marriage under consideration at all. That and the fact you keep holding back on me, not letting me know about you. I want to find out. Of course you love me, Fox.''

"I really do,'' he pleaded. "Marry me.''

He said it to someone who had just fallen asleep. It was as if her telling him how he felt about her had done it to her. Like his love was some special pill that made her feel everything was all right with the world. He loved her: therefore she fell into a peaceful, happy sleep. Like pills it would be hard to break the habit. Fox should have understood that. If he had he might have fallen asleep, too. Instead he ended up staring at the black ceiling, staring and staring, and listening to the nighttime sirens of the city shriek through his windows.

"I'll settle for living with you," Fox said at breakfast.

Kim Hartman was reading the newspaper. Bright light was on her face. Her clean, fine cheekbones were highlighted, and she looked very beautiful.

"Don't give up all hope," she said. "Don't give up so easily. I think I need glasses."

"Glasses?"

"I'm having trouble reading the fine print. When does it happen, Fox, when do you become farsighted? Do you think I'll be farsighted and a grandmother by next year? I suppose it's possible. Robert is certainly capable of knocking up some girl."

"I want to talk some more about what we were discussing last night," Fox said. "I stayed awake a long time thinking about it."

"You did? Poor Fox," Kim said. She reached out and took his hand and kissed it, all the time still reading.

"I'm emotionally exhausted by it," she said. "I need some time to think. I'd like to know, for example, how come someone as nice as you isn't married by now, or hasn't been divorced. Will you tell me that sometime, but definitely not now."

"Sometime," Fox said.

Kim Hartman put down the newspaper, folding it neatly. "Well," she said, "shall we get under way? Shall we go to work?"

It wasn't really a question because she stood up as she said it. Fox was a little slower.

"Let's get going, Robert," she said.

"Robert?"

"I did a little thinking too," Kim Hartman said. "I don't think it helps you to be called Fox by me. Everyone in the law firm calls you Fox. Now that is perfectly normal in a law firm, but not in a love affair. I am going to do my part to contribute to making this thing work."

35

THERE ARE SO many people on Wall Street. Fox tended to forget that all these people had faces, and was only reminded of that if some friend tapped him on the shoulder. This morning Wall Street was overcast, the black clouds hovering over the canyon, ready to collapse on it.

And this morning Fox met another New York phenomenon, caused because there are so many people. He met the stare. The stare is given when the man thinks he knows you, but can't place the face. This man wore a blue topcoat, his skin was richly tan, and he looked so innocent and totally in control that Fox never gave him a second thought. But as Fox tried to slip past, the man who had stopped and was staring at Fox grabbed his shoulder.

"Jack?" he said.

Fox was pretty sure he didn't know the man, but not totally sure. How can you be, in New York?

"Don't I know you?" the man said. "I must know you from somewhere."

"I don't think so," Fox said.

"Oh I know you, all right," the man said, half turning his face, looking at Fox as if there were an invisible microscope between them. "I know you. Your face. Sure, it's been a long time. Jack Bender."

"Fox," Fox said. "Robert Fox."

"Fox?"

"That's my name," he said. He gently took the man's hand off his shoulder.

The well-dressed gentleman stood quietly in the flow of bodies, mulling things over. Jack Bender? Robert Fox? He was a man trying to get in touch with his past, Fox thought. You lose your past here in this city, despite what Kim says about it coming back to haunt you.

Fox got to his office, took off his coat, and was going to plan his day. He never got a chance.

"Mrs. Sifford called you," Miss Algur said. "She is agitated."

Mrs. Sifford? For a second Fox thought the secretary was talking about old dead Mrs. Sifford. She meant, of course, the wife of Charles Sifford, Jr.

"Shall I get her on the line?"

"Yes, Algur." Algur was very efficient and Mrs. Sifford appeared to have been sitting by the phone.

Either that or she could really move in her tennis shoes.

"Mr. Fox," she said, and paused. There was a sort of resignation in her voice, and the tone also implied that somehow Fox had caused some trouble. But there was something else too: she'd paused to pull herself together.

"We had a visit from a lunatic this morning," she said, very deliberately. "And you promised that you would handle everything." She paused again. Lunatic? Fox thought. It had to have been a bad lunatic for this nurse to lose her self-control.

"I have been thinking out exactly what I would tell you, Mr. Fox." Now she seemed to have calmed down: the professional tone was there. "I could tell you nothing. Or I could tell you everything. I have decided to tell you everything for two reasons. The first is that I don't want to live with it. And the second is that my husband is disturbed." She said husband so that the word sounded exactly like patient. "I'm also afraid that if I don't tell you, and you do not clean up this mess, more things will happen. Finally, I'm telling you because I need help."

"I understand," Fox said very calmly.

"You do not understand, Mr. Fox," she said. "But it doesn't matter."

"What happened?" Fox said, thinking: Keep her on track, get the story before her emotions take over again.

"Apparently old Marsiglia has been keeping some sort of lunatic locked up in his house. I think—I'm sure—his son brought the man up here. I've got no idea how long he's been there, but I can recognize the signs of delirium tremens, detoxification, and madness. I know those very well. The man escaped. He should be in a hospital, Mr. Fox. The man is very, very sick.''

So Marsiglia sent Martin Beard to his father. Who else could he trust? Fox thought. Who could he trust completely who lived far enough away and would not tell anyone a damn thing: his father. Well, so Marsiglia doesn't kill people. Interesting. He didn't kill Martin Beard after all. Jackson was wrong.

''Do you understand everything so far, Mr. Fox?''

''Yes,'' Fox said. ''The man's name is Martin Beard, Mrs. Sifford. He worked for your husband's father.''

''I know all that, Mr. Fox,'' she said sternly. It's her story, Fox thought. Keep your mouth shut.

''My husband recognized him. It was a very disagreeable meeting. The lunatic staggered through our open door, and he threw himself on my husband. He clutched my husband, moaning and babbling. This is the hard part, Mr. Fox. The man was babbling about Marsiglia and himself, and about my husband's father. And he was saying that he wanted to be forgiven, but that he wanted money, too. All of this was coming out of him in an insane babbling streak. He wanted forgiveness for what he and Marsiglia had done to my father-in-law, but he wanted money to keep his mouth shut. And sometimes he thought that he actually was my father-in-law, come back to life. Can you understand the position I'm in?''

How had she gotten rid of Beard? Fox was wondering.

''Yes, ma'am.''

''The man clearly had something to do with killing my father-in-law, and clearly Marsiglia had something to do with it too. And Marsiglia's father lives next to us and we *love* him. Can you understand?''

Now she broke down. Fox let her sob and didn't say a thing. What could he say? He would do something, though, because of how she'd said ''love.'' She had said it with great emotion, it had come whooshing out of her in one great burst. Clearly the woman had not married Charles Sifford, Jr., simply for his money. She must love him, too.

''I'm sorry,'' she said when she'd stopped sobbing. ''What is my responsibility? Do I report this to the police?''

''You have no responsibility,'' Fox said. ''I am going to take care of everything. What happened to Mr. Beard?''

''I have given Martin Beard Librium, and dealt with him correctly. He is now lying peacefully asleep in a bedroom. He was a strong one, Mr. Fox—I've seen very strong patients—and I dealt with him firmly, with the correct amount of force, and correctly, at least medically correctly. Should I call the police?''

Why was she so worried about the police? Fox wondered. Was it because she wanted to make very sure that she didn't make any mistakes now that would come back to haunt her, the way Martin Beard had?

"You acted completely properly, Mrs. Sifford," Fox said. "Can you keep him there? Please don't call the police. I am fully responsible. Can you do that? Are you capable of that?"

"Of course," she said firmly.

"Will it upset your husband?"

"My husband has come back a long way, Mr. Fox. I will handle him. But the lunatic needs hospitalization."

"He'll get it," Fox said. "An ambulance will be there soon."

"I'm exhausted, Mr. Fox. Please get a fast ambulance."

"I will. Thank you," Fox said. "You've done everything perfectly and I will report any developments to you."

"You don't understand!" she said, almost screaming. "We don't want any developments. We don't want to be told anything. We just want to live in peace."

"I'm going to see that you can," Fox said.

36

JACKSON LOOKED VERY, very tired and seemed cranky, and that made Fox wonder again about what was happening to him, but he didn't ask. There wasn't time.

"There's going to be an ambulance outside in about ten minutes, Jackson," Fox began.

"Do I look that bad?"

A joke, Fox thought, Jackson made a joke. Wonderful. Now he's becoming human, just when I need him to act efficiently, like the robot he used to be.

"This is important, Jackson," Fox said. "I'm going to do the talking, and you're going to take a trip, and not make any jokes."

"Sorry," Jackson said, looking as if he would never tell another joke.

"I liked your joke," Fox said. "I intend to take you to dinner as a reward for it, but not just now. There isn't time. Outside, my secretary is typing up some directions. You are going to get in your ambulance, drive full-tilt up along the Hudson River, and pick up a lunatic who is at the house of Charles Sifford, Jr. Do you understand?"

Jackson looked baffled: Harvard Law School.

Clerking on the third circuit. Hours and hours in the classroom. A perfect A average. The result: picking up lunatics. "Yes," he said dejectedly. "I guess so."

"You are going to put your lunatic in your ambulance, with the help of Mrs. Sifford and the attendant who is going with you, and you are going to check the lunatic in at Broadmoor."

"Broadmoor?" Jackson said.

"Broadmoor is another one of those great Hudson River estates, Jackson, pretty much on the order of what you're going to see at the Sifford house. Only the owner of Broadmoor lost all his money in the Depression, and it is now what is politely called a rest home by all the rich people in New York. What it does, however, is reform the occasional truant client who has become an alcoholic or a mental case. It also takes in the occasional best-selling author who has gone nuts, or Pulitzer Prize–winning eccentric poet who is having trouble, but I don't have time to explain it all to you. You'll see for yourself."

"I *leave* the lunatic at Broadmoor?" Jackson said hopefully.

"That's right. You don't have to stay with him. I'm not hospitalizing you yet. I am going to call Broadmoor while you are in your ambulance, and they will take care of everything. They are very, very efficient.

"And quiet. Your lunatic is going to be very quiet too, because Mrs. Sifford, who happens to be a nurse, has given him a lot of Librium. You don't have a thing to worry about."

"Then why do I have to go?" Jackson said. "Why can't you just send the ambulance?"

My God, Fox thought, now Jackson is actually objecting to direct orders. It's wonderful. Jackson is now almost a complete human like me.

"You are going because I am telling you to," Fox said. "Do you understand?"

"Or I get fired?"

"Yes, Jackson, or you get fired. Sorry. Just when I was beginning to like you too. Listen, I want you there to make absolutely sure that nothing goes wrong. I don't think it will, but it might. Anything is possible. Marsiglia probably knows by now that the lunatic is in the Sifford house, and he wants him too."

"Wait a minute," Jackson said. "Marsiglia offs people."

Ten minutes, Fox thought, looking at his watch, and we've eaten up eight of them. What was he going to do about Jackson? Should he send someone else? No. There wasn't time now to explain it to another person.

"Jackson, don't use the words *off people* in this office. Please. It makes me nervous. It just isn't done. Don't talk about murder or police. I told you we were a stodgy firm. If you want to make partner, you just can't say things like off people. Besides that, Jackson, Marsiglia does *not* off people. I haven't put the whole thing together yet, but that is one thing I know for a fact. If he did, Martin Beard would not be alive."

"Oh God," Jackson yelled, "not Martin Beard. Not again."

"Yes, Jackson. Martin Beard. *Your* lunatic."

Jackson had a hand up over his face. Life is tough all over, Fox thought. Gauder had once sent me into a rat-infested one-room, windowless apartment, where an old lady had lain dead for ten days before anyone noticed and called the police.

The old lady happened to be worth eight million dollars, and they proved it by what Fox found in his search, which was conducted in a suit, but with a surgical mask over his face to cut the incredible smell in the place.

What did Jackson have to complain about?

"Maybe Marsiglia has learned his lesson, and decided to improve his methods," Jackson said.

"Start moving," Fox told him. *Sternly.*

Jackson started to get up, very, very slowly. Fox was about to really let Jackson have it, but then he thought of something else, so he was glad Jackson had taken his time.

"What do we call him?" Fox asked Jackson.

"Who?"

"Your lunatic. He's got to have a name."

"Don't ask me." Jackson looked miserable.

"All right," Fox said. "We'll call him Jackson, Mr. Jackson. Now move. Or you're fired. Tell the people at Broadmoor that Mr. Jackson gets no visitors unless I say so."

Jackson gave up all resistance and moved. Not too fast. But at least he got on his way. Well, he's not driving the ambulance, Fox thought, he'll get into the whole thing when they begin blowing the siren. And Fox smiled. *Broadmoor.* For the first time in its life, it was going to welcome a servant, not a master.

About time, Fox thought. Then, he got started on the phone, explaining how another of his firm's clients had had an unfortunate attack, and needed complete care and supervision, absolute isolation from anyone, and no contacts with the outside world. Mr. Jackson, Fox told them, was from Orlando, Florida, and worth millions, and, yes, Fox went all the way, and lied, and told them he had Mr. Jackson's power of attorney.

There was only one thing Fox regretted. If there had been more time, he could have told Broadmoor that Mr. Jackson, the patient, was coming in the care of his son, young Jackson, an attorney. But, unfortunately, he hadn't had the time to explain that to the real Jackson.

Jackson called at about three that afternoon. He was connected directly to Fox, who was sitting in a partnership meeting listening to Richard Lovett give another tirade about letting Gauder keep his office.

"We are supposed to retire at sixty-five, and for good reason." The "good reason" was that the old man did not hit the urinal, Lovett argued.

All the associate lawyers imagine we sit at these meetings discussing their futures and evaluating them, Fox thought. If they only knew what we really talk about: new business and urinals. The call came directly through to Fox as ordered. He used Jackson as an excuse, left the meeting, and spoke to Jackson in his own office.

"*My* lunatic is at Broadmoor," Jackson said.

"And I'm about to take *my* ambulance home, unless you've decided that I'm supposed to walk."

Fantastic, Fox thought, we've won. Now it all unravels. If Martin Beard can manage to stay alive. Hell, they'll keep him alive at Broadmoor.

"*Am* I supposed to walk?" Jackson snapped.

"You've done a great job," Fox said. "Really. Thank you."

"All I did was ride in an ambulance. Which I absolutely refuse to do again, unless it's for my own health and safety. Go ahead and fire me. Why do I get all the shit work? Aren't there any other associates at the firm you can dump on? Why do you hate me? What did I do?"

"Calm down," Fox said. "Just lie down in the ambulance and sleep your way home."

"Other associates get assigned decent work. They get to learn something. Even if it's only tax law. You assign me Martin Beard. I quit."

"You're just upset," Fox said. "And you don't realize that what you've done is very important, and that you've been learning some very important things. Now, get in the ambulance and go to sleep."

"Sleep? Sleep?" Jackson was screaming so loud that Fox had to hold the phone away from his ear, even though it was a long-distance call. "I haven't slept in a week. Don't you understand? I have problems of my own. And on top of all that, I've got you. I thought this was a prestigious firm. I thought I would learn something. I thought I might find the work enjoyable. Now nothing is going right. Sleep? *I hate you.*"

"Jackson, please," Fox said, "don't yell, and

don't say the name Martin Beard out loud again. I don't want the people at Broadmoor to hear that name.''

Now Jackson really let go: it was as if his whole insides came spilling out. What little he had left of them.

''Do you think I'm stupid? Why is that? Why do you continually treat me like an idiot? I did better than you did at Harvard. I was on the *Law Review.* You were in the middle of your class, and on top of it you were kicked out of prep school. Don't you understand anything about me? I am calling from a *phone booth.* Got it?''

''I *am* sorry, Jackson,'' Fox said. ''Listen, I want to know all about your personal problems, so we'll sit down and talk about them. We'll have a long talk. Come home.''

''Home? You think working with you is like being at 'home'? It's like being institutionalized at Broadmoor. And you want to know something? They asked if I was Martin Beard's son!''

Fox hung up on him. What else could he do? Perfect Jackson would probably lose the rest of his stomach after being considered the son of a lunatic, but at least he was in an ambulance. He'll calm down, Fox thought. And I will find out what's bugging him. I'll make him tell me.

And how did he find out about the prep school thing? How do associates find out everything about partners? I've got to get Jackson back in line, he thought. I'm going to need him. Now it is all going to break loose.

PART FOUR

The Fisherwoman

37

WHEN MARSIGLIA finally got on the line, there was a great whooshing whistling sound in the background. He's probably up on the top of one of his buildings, Fox thought. One that's going up, standing on a girder. Does he have some hard-hat who follows him around with a telephone in a rivet bucket?

"I know what you want," Marsiglia said.

"I thought you also ought to know that I've got Martin Beard," Fox said.

"I said I knew what you wanted," Marsiglia shouted into the phone. "I know all that. Why do you think I'm talking to you?"

"I want to meet you," Fox said. "Now."

"Not now," Marsiglia answered him. "We'll talk tomorrow. I'll pick you up. We'll talk at ten."

"Now," Fox said.

He wanted to start cracking things open. By ten tomorrow, Marsiglia might have gotten Beard out of Broadmoor. How much did Marsiglia actually know? How much power did he have?

"I can't hear you well," Marsiglia shouted. "The wind. Understand? I can't stop the wind. We'll talk at ten tomorrow. I'll pick you up and that's the way it is."

"No," Fox said. "That is not the way it is. Now."

"What are you so goddamned impatient for?" Marsiglia shouted against the wind. "It's waited these thirteen damned years, and it can wait one more day. I know what you know. I know all about Beard and where you've got him, and I know all about you. Learn some patience."

Then Marsiglia hung up on Fox.

There were a lot of things Fox could have done. He thought for a long time about whether he ought to do any of them. He decided not to do anything. Marsiglia was right: it had waited thirteen years, and it could wait one more day. Besides, Gauder would have waited. Fox felt it in his bones. Gauder would have waited because Marsiglia had not, as Jackson liked to say, offed Beard. Besides, there's Jackson, Fox thought. I owe him another good dinner, a long talk, and more help: I should teach him a little more than how to handle a lunatic, so I'll explain everything to him, and get him really talking.

It was about five, and Jackson was due back soon. The telephone rang, the call was put through directly, and Kim Hartman said: "Now you can come to *my* apartment."

Well, perhaps Jackson needed sleep more than a long talk with Fox.

"Tonight?"

"I mean tonight, yes." She sounded giddy. "Pronto. I want you here. And don't bother to tell me that there is anything pressing at the office."

Nothing pressing, Fox thought, just a lunatic in Broadmoor, one murder, and three million dollars missing. If anything came up during the night, Jackson could handle it.

"Nothing pressing."

"The only thing I don't have is the champagne," she said. "I need it. Would you get the good stuff?"

"What is the good stuff?" Fox asked.

"Moët, you boob. Don't you know anything? Don't you ever drink anything other than Scotch?"

"I'll do just what you say," Fox said, writing down Moët carefully in his appointment book, and at the same time standing up and trying to get his jacket on, still holding the phone.

"Is there anything else?" Kim said. "Let's see. Is there?" Fox got the jacket on.

"Why am I asking you?" Kim said. "You wouldn't know anyway."

And then she hung up on Fox, like everyone else.

Fox got two bottles of Kim's special champagne, even though it was incredibly expensive. And he carried them to Kim Hartman's door, and rang the bell. Instead of inviting him in, she came out, closing the door behind her. She was smiling. What teeth, Fox thought, perfect pearl teeth. And what pearls. The ones I gave her. Pearls? Champagne? Kim Hartman is costing me a bundle, and I'll probably get dumped.

"I thought I was going to get to go inside for a change," Fox said.

She took the bottles from him.

"You are, Fox. You are. But be patient. I want you to put your hands over your eyes. I will lead you into my apartment."

She really *was* giddy, and finally she just laughed: it sounded crazy, and wonderful, and manic. All the things that Fox was not, which was one of the many reasons he loved her.

"Hands over eyes?" he said. "This is some sort of surprise party?"

"No guessing," Kim said. "Close your eyes, put your hands over them, and no cheating."

Fox did it. He was, after all, madly in love with her.

"All right," he said. "And I'm not cheating."

"I didn't think you were. You can take them off again and open your eyes," she told him, and let go of his arm.

"But I'm not inside," Fox said. "What's the problem?"

"The problem is that I just locked myself out. I am hysterical tonight."

That's all right, Fox thought, everyone else appears to be too. Jackson, Gauder, Martin Beard, the younger Mr. Sifford, Mrs. Banning, Marsiglia. No,

Fox thought, he's not. Too bad. Fox never asked himself whether *he* was in top mental shape.

"Do something, Fox," Kim said. "Get the manager, you boob, please."

Boob? Fox felt the way Jackson felt all the time.

"Kim, I've got a key. Right in my pocket. You gave it to me."

"Oh good," she said. "Yes."

He handed her the key, and resumed his position with his hands over his closed eyes. And he didn't cheat. Kim Hartman got the door open, and pulled Fox into her apartment. There were steps, and he had to move carefully. There was also no carpeting. Fox did not notice that until he almost tripped on the rug.

"Can I open my eyes?" he asked. "Please."

"You are a good wonk, Fox," Kim said. "You haven't cheated even though you almost killed yourself. Just a little farther, please."

"You said you were going to call me Robert," Fox said.

"I've changed my mind. I'll tell you why later. Now, Mr. Fox, you may open your big brown orbs."

He opened them. *She had turned the apartment into the Ardeonuig Hotel!* The floors were lemon-colored wood, and looked soft as sand. The rug was soft and off-white. The conversation pit was gone. There was furniture, and it was relaxed light brown rattan, with white pillows. The last yellow edge of sunset poured in through the windows.

"Well?"

"Great," Fox said.

"That's it? Great? I finally make some real decision about how I want things, and what makes me feel good, and all you can say is great?''

Actually great *was* all that Fox could say. He did not use words like fantastic, wonderful, marvelous, stupendous, superb. They didn't exist in his mind. If they had, he would have gotten along better with Kim Hartman.

"Terrific," Fox said, groping, trying as hard as he could and finally coming up with something. "This must have cost you a bundle."

"It did," she said. "I don't care. I love it, and it's fantastic, and I've created a whole new style: basic Ardeonuig Hotel. I didn't go all the way. I did use Formica in the kitchen. And I kept the mirrors."

Mirrors? Fox wondered.

"I kept the mirrors in the bedroom," Kim Hartman said. "Because they're sort of fun." And she giggled.

The mirrors *were* sort of fun. And Fox had taken a peek or two as they made love. Now they lay quietly together, with their eyes closed.

"So the twit was the decorator?" Fox said.

"He's not a twit," she murmured. "And I'm not having an affair with anyone. He is a very good decorator, and a fast one, and he understood everything I wanted. He is also a friend, and his crew worked around the clock as a special favor for me, because I send him business. By the way, I think he's been to the hotel. He understood too well."

"And why won't you call me Robert?"

"I can't call you Robert because there are too

many Roberts in my life, all of them ghosts, and it cost me fifty thousand dollars in analyst time to exorcise them, Fox. I don't want another Robert. My father is named Robert, and my brother, my son, and my ex-husband. Which is probably why I married him in the first place. Now you know." She sat up, as if all this disturbed her.

"I think I'll get my one cigarette," she said. "Or did I have it?"

"You didn't have it," Fox said. "We haven't even eaten dinner."

"You're right," she said. "I got carried away. The redecoration made me manic. When I knew what I wanted, I wanted it *right now*."

She *had* gotten carried away: Fox had picked her up and carried her into the bedroom. His back was killing him. She had *demanded* to be carried. He got her cigarettes.

"I'm forty, Fox," she said, "and I've got to do what's good for me. Why do I always think I can't?" Fox lit the cigarette. Kim's hand shook as he held up the flame. And suddenly, it hit him: she's about to tell me she's not going to marry me. Too many Roberts in her life.

"Fox," she said, "I can't do what's good for you, or for Fluffy, or for anyone. I want to do what's good for me. Do you understand? So I'm going to call you Fox. Is that all right?"

"Great," Fox said.

"Even thinking about all those Roberts makes me nervous, so I'm going to call you Fox, and not think about any of them." She paused.

Don't do it, Fox pleaded in his mind, exorcise

them, but not me. This Robert is alive, living, caring. He loves you.

"I love you," she said. Thank God, Fox thought.

She snuffed out the cigarette, which she had not even bothered to put in her mouth, and snuggled down next to him. She was tall, but very thin, so that when she snuggled down, it was as if she was a tiny thing, Fox thought, a wonderful tiny woman.

"Let's change the subject, Fox," she said. "You talk. About your mother and then about the first time you made love."

Fox was thinking, Yes, let's change the subject, and thank God, at least she hadn't made up her mind yet. Yes, change the subject, this isn't the time.

"Or you could talk about why you are thirty-six, and not married yet," she added. "You have lots to tell me."

He hadn't said anything, was still just coming down off the tingling sensation he'd had when he thought she was about to dump him. Now she put her hand up and placed her finger up to his lips and slowly moved her finger around his lips, just barely touching them. It was a very sexy feeling.

"Talk, Fox," she whispered as she did it.

"All right," he said. "But not about Mom, or any of that. No ghosts. Give me a break. All right?"

He meant: don't give me a breakdown. To avoid one, he told her about Jackson's transformation from robot to crazed lunatic attendant.

They had finally gotten up to eat dinner, and were drinking the champagne with it.

"Jackson is crazed because he has been rejected

by Miss Fluffy Ravenel,'' Kim Hartman explained. ''I know the entire story. It is impossible to keep Fluffy from babbling. She actually cried as she explained it all to me.''

''But they've only known each other a week or two.''

''They made love the first day they met. I mean: that night.''

Fox had known Kim Hartman for well over two months before they had made love. And she had had so much trouble making up her mind about it that he had never been sure they were actually going to do it until it was over.

''Fluffy talks Southern,'' Kim went on, ''and claims she does exactly what her daddy tells her to do, but she's hard as steel. Jackson didn't fit into her game plan. She's having too much fun. So good-bye Jackson. Fluffy goes out every night, to all the places you read about. She doesn't have time for Jackson. Fluffy knows when she's going to get married, when she's going to have children, and how many. Seriously, I sometimes think she's plotting to take over my business.''

Let her, Fox thought, and we'll get married.

''Actually, I want to go out to some of those places myself, Fox. Take me,'' Kim Hartman said. ''I just want to see what's going on. There's some place called CBGB's? Have you been there? Apparently, the Ramones have.''

''The what?'' Fox said.

''The Ramones. Fluffy is nuts about them. They are some kind of demented adolescents who play the kind of music that I grew up on. And it is all

199

extremely chic. In Fluffy's crowd. Sometimes I think things may have turned full circle. I've got to go out and see for myself. Fluffy claims the Ramones are straight fifties. Maybe they're her fifties. I doubt they're mine."

Things aren't full circle, Fox thought. They made love the first time they met.

Kim Hartman poured Fox some of his champagne. The fact was that Fox could not tell the difference between this and any other champagne. There was a difference, of course, and Kim could tell it with a sniff.

"Fluffy loves to make love. I think affairs are her hobby. She claims to be an art expert, but I think her real business is love."

"Sex," Fox said.

"She gets them confused. She claims she did actually love Jackson. It was apparently very hard for her to dump him. So she claims. But apparently Jackson is just not right for her. He's too serious. He doesn't even drink."

"I think he gave it a try for her sake," Fox said, and explained about Jackson's stomach.

"I'm sorry he ran into Fluffy," Kim said. "She can really put it away. I have to go out and see some of the things she babbles about. The most exotic thing we've done is go to Couples."

Kim Hartman had pushed Fox very hard for that. He had finally done it, with great reluctance. The experience had been excruciating. You paid about fifty dollars for a piece of meat you could not see in the dark, and listened to music that made it impossible for you to talk.

"Will you take me, Fox?"

He thought: if you marry me.

"Sure," he said: it might all come down to that.

"I guess this making love all the time, and on the first night, is a sort of holdover from the sixties, Fox," she said. "That's the only way I can understand it. Of course, I never understood the sixties, but you can explain that all to me sometime. Right now let's get into bed together with the rest of our champagne. All right?"

It was always all right with Fox. It was great. But he wasn't that much younger than Kim. He wasn't really a flower child. He would have to find one and pump him for information on the sixties.

"You know my apartment feels so comfortable now, so relaxed and just plain good, that I feel as if I'm taking Valium. But I'm not. No ghosts can get in here. That is how I feel."

It made Fox feel the same: he fell into a peaceful sleep undisturbed by the fact that he had to meet Marsiglia in the morning and deal with real ghosts.

38

AT EXACTLY ten o'clock, Miss Algur informed Fox that Mr. Marsiglia was on the telephone. "I'm waiting for you," Marsiglia said.

"Where?" he asked.

"Right in front of your building," Marsiglia said.

It was a beautiful day and Fox didn't need his coat. He didn't need his briefcase either. All he needed were his brains, and some of the training Gauder had given him. As he walked out, the sun poured in the glass doors on the ground level of Fox's building.

Outside a huge black Cadillac was parked in a no-parking zone. The car shone in the sun, and looked like a hearse. Marsiglia has got himself all dressed up as if he were the Godfather, Fox thought. Then the driver, who wore a uniform, sprung out to open the door for Fox. The driver was a woman: a pretty, young girl. She looked great in the semi-TWA outfit. Just as if Fox was getting on a plane. That made Fox feel a lot better. He did not believe that Marsiglia would off him with a woman around. He must have learned at least that much from the Siffords. The door thunked shut and the car started moving.

There was energy. At first Fox thought it was just his own nervousness. Then slowly he realized it was more than that. Marsiglia had a presence that was concentrated in his eyes. The face was ordinary, plain. But the black eyes that bore in on Fox seemed to lock on target as if somewhere inside them were the cross hairs of a rifle scope. The man could *concentrate*. And now his black eyeballs locked in on Fox's own eyes, and there was energy that seemed to dance an invisible path between the two men.

"Good morning," Fox said.

The eyes stayed locked in place. Marsiglia said nothing.

"Why is it necessary to have this conversation in your car?" Fox prodded.

"It *isn't necessary,*" Marsiglia said. "I like to drive. *Understand?*"

Gauder had trained Fox to listen carefully: let the other person talk, and then think very hard about what they are *really* saying. "I like to drive?" What did Marsiglia mean? Fox was very nervous and thought very hard, and then he understood.

Old Mr. Meecham, the railroad baron, who had come from nowhere, and built a fortune, had loved to blast up the banks of the Hudson River in his train. There was a connection: the founders, the originals, who started the money river flowing, all "liked to drive," and were all a little strange too, there was no doubt about that. Marsiglia's car was strange: a huge black Cadillac with everything in it: a small Sony

203

color television, a telephone. A pretty woman driver, in her uniform. It was a little much, and eccentric. The only people who drove around in big black Cadillacs like this, as far as Fox knew, were the television people at Black Rock, and they only did so occasionally. When some star was in town. It just was not a part of what was done in New York by intelligent people. Even the Mafia used rented Fords. Why stuff a body in an expensive clean Cadillac? Well, Marsiglia probably *does* know that, Fox thought. He just doesn't give a damn. He likes to drive, so he does it.

Marsiglia doesn't give a damn, but his children will, Fox thought. He will send them to private schools and to the best colleges. And they would flow with the money, learning manners all the time, generation after generation, until they didn't like to drive anymore. And then they would lose the money. The river of money would find a new bed, would be diverted, just as it had been diverted from the Siffords to Marsiglia, who was building New York now with it, just the way old original, eccentric Mr. Meecham had. Suddenly Fox realized this was important. I'm right here, watching the change, getting to see it all, see how the city works. The great Hudson River flows down to the city. It is a river of gold. The color of Kim Hartman's hair. The color of a life preserver. The color Frederick Church used in his exploding sunsets.

"Why won't you tell me about Mrs. Sifford," Fox said.

"I don't tell anyone anything unless I have to,"

Marsiglia grunted. "I have to now, or I have to kill people."

Marsiglia *is* very, very smart. He does understand how it works, and where you draw the line, Fox thought. The river of money may stay with the Marsiglias for a long time.

"And I'm not just talking about Martin Beard," Marsiglia added. "But you know that, don't you? I'm talking about the others. What have you got with Martin Beard? A madman. That's all. Nothing. Who cares what he says?"

Fox said nothing. Marsiglia was partly right and partly wrong. And Marsiglia knew it.

"And you would never find old Mr. Sifford," Marsiglia said. "So there is nothing there either. But the others, you would play them against each other some way. And I would get caught, somehow. You want your particular three million dollars. I know all about you. You're smart enough."

"Yes," Fox said. "Mrs. Sifford's particular three million."

"She killed him," Marsiglia said. "After she had prayed all night, thinking about it. I wasn't there, or I might have stopped her."

"Who killed him?" Fox asked quietly because Marsiglia had said "she" in a soft reverential way.

"Old Mrs. Sifford, she killed him. And I put him under the building. I moved him with Beard. Who else was there but Beard? And then I finished the building. The Blagden Building. All this time Banning has been living right over him, and she doesn't know a thing about it. Mrs. Sifford caught them in bed, Banning ran, and then Mrs. Sifford went to her room and prayed all day. The next evening, she shot him dead. She came from a different generation. And she would have given me the money to finish the building," Marsiglia added, "I'm sure of it. I think she would have given it to me if she hadn't caught her husband. It was hell for her."

"Why?" Fox asked.

"Because she believed in God. There are people who do," Marsiglia said, suddenly his voice booming. "She believed in God, and also in the righteous power of God's revenge. She wanted revenge, but she wanted to go to heaven, too. When she shot him, she knew she was going to go to hell. Understand? That is why she lived so long. She didn't want to go to hell."

Fox remembered the way old Mrs. Sifford had looked in death: fighting it all the way. Marsiglia was right: Mrs. Sifford did come from a different generation. It meant a little more when that generation told someone to go to hell.

"I don't have to tell you all this," Marsiglia said. "I tell you because I want you to do it right. If you don't understand, you can't play it right. You're not going to do anything to me. What have you got? A lunatic. And a corpse that is down four stories in the ground, with forty-eight more built over him. You think they're going to tear down the building?"

"You thought I was going to go to the police?" Fox said, astonished. "Indict you as an accessory to murder?"

"I know everything about you," Marsiglia said. "So I didn't think so. But it took me some time to find out. Why do I tell you this?"

Because you have to, Fox thought. They were out on the East Side, along the river. It looked surprisingly clean in the bright sunlight.

"You're looking for exactly three million two. Aren't you, Mr. Fox?"

"Yes," Fox said.

"Here is a list of the investors who went in on the Blagden Building. You'll see that Banning came in for exactly three million two. Your particular three million two, Mr. Fox. It has to be. But I never knew she'd stolen the money from Mrs. Sifford. She said she'd gotten the money from her wealthy friends. That was why she was using so many little companies in order to make the investment. If there had been another way, I never would have taken the money from her. Banning is crazy, dangerous. I don't like my investors that way. I like them quiet. I never let her come in on another project. But I was desperate. Don't use the paper unless you have to, and don't get me in the newspapers. Just take the money from her quietly. Understand?"

Fox understood perfectly: it was exactly what he planned to do.

"How crazy is she?" he said.

"Who the hell knows how crazy anyone is? Look at me: I look out at this city, and wherever there's an empty space I see a big building in it. Banning's crazy, and sick on top of it. But she used to be very smart. She invested in me. If she's still smart she'll just give you back your little three million and live on the rest. I made her a lot. She used to be smart. I mean, she got the money away from Mrs. Sifford. And you'll find out who helped her."

"Yes." Of course, for Christ sake, he thought, she had to have someone to vouch for her.

"What do we do with Beard?" Marsiglia said suddenly. And then he answered his own question. "Leave him at Broadmoor. Tell them to send me the bills. I've got his power of attorney anyway. I'll worry about him. I've been doing it thirteen damn years."

"All right," Fox said. Why not? Let Martin Beard babble away at Broadmoor with some of the friends and some of the distant relatives of the Sifford family themselves. It didn't make any difference. All that really counted now was how dangerous and crazy Mrs. Banning was.

They had gone north, along the East River, and then across town, on the Hudson River Drive, and then taken the fast exit, twisted through two small streets, and they were on the West Side Highway, or what was left of it, the Hudson River now on their right. So we're going to circle Manhattan, Fox thought, as if Marsiglia owned the entire place, as if he is like some land baron, inspecting his town.

"If you have to, you can call on me for help," Marsiglia said. "I hate most people, but I belong to every goddamned thing that I'm allowed to. I never go to the meetings. I contribute to everything. I don't ask the name of the organization. I don't care. I give to the politicians, and I don't vote. So I have some favors outstanding."

Fox was talking to a man who had covered up murder. But it was a special kind, he reminded himself.

"You know what I can do," Marsiglia said.

"Thank you," Fox said. "How did you get Mr. Sifford under the building?"

He really wanted to know. It was just curiosity. He didn't come across this kind of case very often.

"Why?" Marsiglia asked.

"It doesn't matter," Fox said. "I apologize."

"I put him in a crate, and I got a truck, with Beard, and took him to the construction site. You think I'm the kind of builder who puts in peepholes so that the public can look at what I'm doing? To hell with the public."

"Did your construction people think it was funny?" Fox asked.

"They aren't paid to think. They build. But it was at night. Just a guard. I told him to go away. Then Beard and I set the box in a hole and poured some concrete. You just press a button."

"Your construction people or the guard didn't think it was strange that in the night the boss had come and poured concrete?"

Fox was thinking: what would happen if all the tenants knew that their building was one giant tombstone for Charles Sifford? Would they want to move? Or would the building become very fashionable?

"I do it all the time," Marsiglia snapped. "When I can't sleep, I go and build. But I tell you, I never built a building as fast as that one. I feel like I lifted that one up with my own two arms. It wasn't just the fact that I had run short of money. I had to cover him up. You ever think about where to put a body? Throw it in the river? That is what they do. Then it floats back to you."

Marsiglia stopped looking out the window, and

stared straight ahead. What's he thinking? Fox wondered. That even though the Blagden Building was huge, sometime another fast boy would tear it down, and sometime the body would come floating back? That would not happen for years, Fox thought. Marsiglia doesn't have to worry. But he must anyway, Fox thought.

Now they were under the crumbling West Side Highway, under the part that was no longer used, and to their right were wharves that were falling into the river, and the buildings were all in tatters. Bums staggered on the dark piers. Then they shot out from under the highway, and the towers of Wall Street were right ahead of them, looking fine in the sun.

"Could you let me out around the Trade Center?" Fox said. "I want to walk." He meant that he wanted to think. Walking, for Fox, was one of his best thinking times. Marsiglia nodded, picked up his telephone, and called the driver. She turned around, smiled behind the glass and nodded. It must work on an intercom, Fox thought, this car has more gadgets than my office. They stopped at the World Trade Center, about a ten-minute walk from Fox's building.

"Farewell," Marsiglia said. The woman had the door open. There was no invitation to shake hands, and Marsiglia was an accessory after the fact to murder, but nevertheless Fox liked him. And hoped he could count on him too.

"Good-bye," Fox said. "Everything is going to be handled very, very quietly."

"That's how I like it, Mr. Fox, but that's not how I see it. Do me one favor, Mr. Fox?"

"Certainly."

"Don't let Mrs. Banning kill you. She's not like Mrs. Sifford. She does not believe in God. But she, too, believes in the righteous power of revenge."

He walked and thought: Old Mrs. Sifford had kicked Mrs. Banning out of her house. Then prayed a day and a night, then killed her husband. Marsiglia and Martin Beard had built the apartment building over him. And Banning knew nothing about it. She had been too busy stealing Mrs. Sifford's money. And Fox had figured out exactly how she had done it. But that did not mean he could get the money back from her easily.

What would Gauder have done? He would have taken the chance and lied, used one lie, and then if that had not worked, he would have used the paper Marsiglia had given him, and really threatened. What could Mrs. Banning do about it? Kill him? Not likely with Randolph around. That boy did not want to be an accessory to murder. From the look of Randolph he wanted, and was waiting for, the chance to take Mrs. Banning's money himself. When she was a little more infirm, when she could no longer walk— then, Fox thought, Randolph would shut her cage door. And if she wanted breakfast or to be carried to the bathroom, he would bring her checkbook and make her sign. Yes, Fox thought, Gauder would have gone directly for the money.

Fox began to feel optimistic on this pretty day, and decided that it was time to take Jackson to lunch. Not dinner. Who could tell about dinner with Kim Hartman around? And in his optimism, weighing everything carefully in his mind, he decided that he would

211

confront Banning directly. He was sure that was what old Gauder would have done. Go directly for the money, not mess around on tangents. We're not detectives, Gauder said. We can't go rushing all around the place. There isn't time for it. We're lawyers, and are paid to think and play our hunches. Fox decided to play his.

39

"WHERE ARE WE going?" Jackson asked. Apparently, he *hadn't* gotten any sleep. He looked worse, Fox thought, and was still grumpy, although he had rescinded his resignation.

"We are going to the Trout Club," Fox told him.

"Isn't that the place that got bombed?" Jackson asked, and stopped in the street. Working with Fox, you ran around in ambulances, and instead of getting taken to a fancy club, went to one that had gotten bombed.

"That is the *other* fishing club," Fox said. "No one is going to bomb the poor old Trout Club."

Was that true? Fox wondered. Who could tell in New York? The other fishing club had indeed been bombed. Some Puerto Rican terrorists had decided to blow up historic old Fraunces Tavern on Wall Street, and the other trout fishing club happened to have its rooms on top of the old tavern. If I was talking to someone from, say, Minnesota, where everything is relatively sane, Fox thought, they would not believe me: in New York, people express their political policies by bombing old taverns and fishing clubs.

Jackson started walking again.

"A long time ago," Fox said, "there were a lot of fishing clubs." He was trying as hard as he could to be nice to Jackson. "And there were also many big private clubs that owned rivers in upstate New York, and you could only fish on those rivers if you were a member. All that is changing, because trout fishing is not fashionable the same way it was. Things have changed a lot. Organizations like Natural Resources Defense Council, which are charitable groups, headed by smart young lawyers"—Fox was going to say, "just like you" and didn't—"are suing, and protecting the rivers. And not for the trout. For the betterment of mankind."

"I know all about organizations like NRDC," Jackson said grumpily. "But who can afford to work for them? They don't pay you any money."

If Jackson had been interested in trout, Fox thought that he could probably have explained the whole history of civilization to Jackson, using trout as a metaphor. There was something in the fact that trout rods had changed from bamboo to fiberglass, and were now made with "high modulous aerospace graphite." Fox, of course, had stuck with bamboo. And he didn't give a damn that the graphite rods could apparently be stomped on by a gorilla and emerge none the worst for wear. There was a lot to trout. A part of the reason that the huge old fishing clubs were disappearing were the changes in the tax laws, but there was also the fact that trout fishing just wasn't what very many rich people wanted to do anymore. Now, Jackson will become a rich person, Fox thought, there is no doubt. What will he want to do in ten years?

"What do you do, Jackson?" Fox asked.

"Do?"

"What's your hobby?"

"It used to be my work."

Have I really been that bad? Fox wondered. "Jackson, what do you do for physical exercise?" Was trout fishing really physical exercise? Fox wasn't sure, but it was very relaxing.

"I play squash and tennis. And if I had any time, I'd go skiing," Jackson said. "I don't run. I think running is stupid."

So did Fox. We have something in common, he thought. Actually, Fox and Jackson had a lot in common, which Fox had not yet recognized, and probably never would. It was why Jackson bothered Fox so much, and why it was difficult for them to work together. Fox had little in common with Kim Hartman, which was why he loved her.

"We agree on something," Fox said. "Jogging is for twits."

They had come to the stairway of the Trout Club. Like the other fishing club, the Trout Club was not huge. It didn't occupy an entire building. It was only one floor of a very old, small building. Luckily, however, the Trout Club owned the small building, and rented out the rest of it. That was how it survived.

Fox buzzed at the door and announced who he was. Before the other fishing club had been bombed, the Trout Club hadn't had a buzzer. You just walked in. But now the members buzzed.

Some of the older, more conservative, and more loony members of the Trout Club believed that there was a conspiracy against fishing clubs. Hadn't one been bombed by Puerto Ricans? Who could tell when they would strike again. Well, maybe they've got a point. Fox's opinion was that anything can happen in New York. He didn't tell Jackson about the buzzer because he wanted Jackson to go up the stairs. The stairs were old, dark, and looked creepy.

"It's not as bad as it looks," Fox said. "It gets better when you get up to the top. It's just an ordinary lunch club."

Was anything ordinary with Fox? Jackson was thinking. How could you trust him? On the other hand, what could Jackson do about it? Unless he quit. He started up the stairs.

It was an ordinary, though old, lunch club. There were the usual big red leather chairs, the dining room with a white linen, a couple of servants, a coat room, a small library, and the rest of it. Things *were* a little seedy. But at least the Trout Club wasn't exclusive. You didn't have to bow to eighteen admission officers to belong.

"See," Fox said. "Just an ordinary club. Nothing unusual. Come and pat the trout."

"Pat the trout?"

"Members and guests pat the trout when they arrive," Fox said. Maybe that did sound strange, Fox realized. He had been doing it so long, he had forgotten how shocked he was when Gauder had first brought him here. "You don't actually have to do it," Fox added. "It's supposed to be lucky, the thing is in a glass case."

It was a monster: a huge fat rainbow trout, caught in eighteen ninety-one, and stuffed. Jackson gave in. Like a zombie, he followed Fox into the library and patted the glass case that held the trout. Then they sat down for lunch.

"There's something I want to say," Jackson said. Fox knew it was something important, because Jackson had violated doctor's orders and drunk half a glass of sherry. Is he going to tell me he was serious about quitting? Fox wondered. Maybe he went out and got himself another job last night.

"I apologize for my behavior after I dropped Mr. Beard at Broadmoor."

"You mean your crank call?" Fox asked. "I've forgotten it."

"It won't happen again," Jackson said stone-faced.

Why can't he accept himself as human and me along with him? Fox thought. I blew my top too after searching that dead lady's room all week. I told Gauder to get lost.

In fact, Fox had not told Gauder to get lost. He had kept all his rage locked up inside himself. But that had been a long time ago, and Fox had sort of switched things around in his memory.

"I'm glad you told me off," Fox said. "I'm glad you got it out of your system. Now, I'd like to talk about what's bothering you."

"I'd rather not," Jackson said. "It's personal."

A man in a white coat was waiting for their orders.

"Trout," Fox said. He looked over at Jackson.

"Steak," Jackson said. "Rare." The man's eyes widened. Then he mumbled something incomprehensible and shuffled away.

"All right," Fox said, "you know a lot about me, well I happen to know a little about you too. And I know about Fluffy."

The mention of Fluffy made Jackson go completely still for a long time. The man in the white coat put the rare steak down in front of a young lawyer who was beginning to have tears form in the corners of his black eyes.

"She just isn't that wonderful," Fox said, thinking this has been a tough week for Jackson's ego, but he's got to face facts.

"She is that wonderful," Jackson said. "I love her."

There are other girls, Fox thought. There are a million Fluffy Ravenels in this world now. "Listen, Jackson, I'm probably going to get dumped myself. And this time it is the right girl, and I actually think I'm in love with her for the right reasons. We all have problems. Please, you can't cry at the Trout Club."

Jackson had let go: the big black sleepless eyes were oozing tears. Actually anyone could cry if he wanted to at the Trout Club, but the idea that Jackson was breaking some mystical rule, like the ritual of patting the trout, or that he was making a fool of himself, seemed to prod him out of his trance. He wiped his face with the napkin, shook his head, and managed to eat a little of his steak. It was then that Fox made the first of his mistakes.

"Jackson, what I've been trying to say is that Miss

217

Ravenel may be cute, but she's also a twit. Actually you're very lucky you got turned down.''

Jackson dropped his fork, his face turned the color of his steak.

''What the hell is wrong with you?'' he shouted. ''Listen, you think she's stupid because she's no neurotic like Kim Hartman? You're making a fool of yourself. First of all, Kim Hartman is too old for you, and secondly, you're right, you are going to ge dumped.''

So he does know all about it!

''I say everything wrong to you,'' Fox babbled. '' can't seem to help it. The truth is that I think Fluffy is very smart, very pretty, but probably isn't inclined to examine herself too closely. You have this way of making me constantly feel I should apologize. Now I'm apologizing, even though I *was* trying to make you feel better.''

They stared at each other.

Jackson shook his head, as if to rattle his brains back into place.

''What's wrong with me?'' he said quietly. ''How did I let her get to me?'' It was as if he'd needed tha final explosion at Fox to ultimately clear his head ''Forget what I said about Kim Hartman. I don' know anything about her except that she's beautiful.''

Fox leaned forward: ''Jackson, you obviously know a good deal, which you learned from Fluffy, and now that we've cleared the air, why don't you tell m what you've heard? Normally, I don't think it's righ to talk about women behind their backs with othe men, but we have a special case here. Don't yo think?''

"Yes," Jackson said, "we always seem to have a special case." And he leaned forward.

"Fluffy says that Kim Hartman acts like a two-year-old. She has no sense of planning. No strategic goals. No master plan. One day she shows up for work. The next day she decides not to come. Fluffy says time is running out on Kim Hartman. No matter how good she looks, she is forty."

"Just what sort of goal should she have?" Fox asked.

"Given Kim Hartman's age bracket, income level, and using population statistics, Fluffy says that Kim Hartman ought to marry you."

"Good," Fox said.

"But she doesn't think Kim Hartman will. After all, there is track record to consider."

"Track record?" Fox asked.

"Kim Hartman hasn't remarried in fifteen years," Jackson said. "I don't know. That's what Fluffy says."

"What about love?" Fox said slowly. "Has Fluffy ever bothered to consider whether or not Mrs. Hartman loves me?"

"Love," Jackson said, looking miserable again. "I tried that argument with Fluffy. I told her I loved her. You know what she said?"

"Jackson, I'm beginning to think our generation gap is as wide as the Hudson River," Fox said. "I have absolutely no idea."

"She said 'talk is cheap.'"

40

"WHEN ARE you coming?" Kim Hartman asked. Fox looked at his watch: it was eight. He had been trying to think through exactly how he was going to play it with Banning, and trying not to think about her.

"Fox," she prodded. "When are you coming home?"

Snap: he was no longer planning his confrontation with Banning. She had said "home," as if they were married, and relieved Fox's tension.

"I'm coming home now," he said.

"Good." She hung up.

Fox got up and started out of the office, wondering whether, if they did get married, things might turn out quite differently than he imagined they would. "You *will* come home," she would tell him then.

On the way out, Fox stopped at Gauder's office. Again, the old man had fallen asleep. Fox closed the door, which was Gauder's open invitation, his way of saying he hoped someone would visit him. Then he gently patted Gauder on the shoulder. Gauder didn't move. Fox kept patting, trying to get hold of it, trying to face the fact that on this night someone else had come to visit Gauder and taken him, carried him off.

I've got to think this through. It's a difficult problem. He sat down in the chair across from Gauder. Outside, he heard the night sounds of the firm: it was only eight, and fast boys were in the library, or chatting quietly in the halls, and secretaries were typing, and the Xerox machines made a very faint hum, all of it blended together.

All right, Fox thought, it's much better this way. He didn't go to an old people's home. He didn't get locked up. And he's not going to hell like Mrs. Sifford. It's much better.

And then he realized he was telling himself a lie. It didn't matter whether Gauder went to an old folks' home or died at the firm: what mattered was *just that he was gone*.

I've got to move, and tell someone about this. The building people will take care of it. They do it all the time. We all look so proper, he thought, that you sometimes forget that death is here, too. And he thought of all the damn people who had committed suicides that were never reported in the press because of the efficiency of the building people, because the owners want things done that way. They want things quiet, just like Marsiglia.

But Fox didn't move. He couldn't. It was slowly welling up inside him, the truth was coming out. It was not like the last time, when Fox's father had died. This time Fox was going to feel it. He could sense it coming, and did not know what to expect. He had been wrapped tight for too long, had placed all his emotions in little neat files in his brain. He actually did not know what he was going to feel. He had forgotten a lot too, just refused to think about it, but now the feeling was coming, a huge cleansing blast of truth, and Fox, as he felt it beginning, did not know what he was facing, and was scared.

It's got nothing to do with the dead body, he thought. Gauder looks as peaceful in death as he had in life. He looks asleep. He just dozed off into it, Fox thought, and then the rolling feeling suddenly hit him.

It hit him physically, altering his entire perception of the world and of himself. He had his head down in his hands and he could not move, or stop the moaning.

Everything he had not done when his father died hit him, and he moaned uncontrollably. It hit him this hard because he now had his father and Gauder all in his mind together. He was moaning for two people, and asking forgiveness for himself, asking why can't it work out right: Why did I not let go then? Why have I been so bad? He blamed himself for his father, and the fact that they had fought and argued, and that he had not loved his father enough. Why hadn't he visited with Gauder more often? A lot of times I took the short way out of the office, left Gauder to fend for himself. And when my father was dying, the visits to the hospital—how many had there been— why had I not been at the hospital when my father died, why? All of it poured out in one surging huge wave, drenching Fox, blasting him, *Gauder, Father, Mother.*

Talk is cheap, Fox thought. But no talk is expensive. Not talking can cost you your life. I didn't talk to him. He didn't tell me. I couldn't talk to him. But I should have tried. There were things I wanted to tell him. He doesn't know. He'll never know. Did I ever tell him I loved him? Did he ever tell me? Why didn't we talk? We had the time. Now, there is no time left.

Fox tried to reach Gauder's telephone and he couldn't. The modern telephone seemed to change as he stared at it, seemed to slowly become the old telephone in the little telephone room of his musty apartment. Old and black. And never ringing. And he had sat there when he was a little boy waiting for the call that never came. Not understanding that the telephone did not ring, because she could not call, because she was dead.

I'm not going to make it, Fox thought, now all of it will not happen, love will not happen, and he felt doomed, marooned and doomed. God, he thought, help them both, take them both, let there be a God, take them and love them. And take me too. What are you doing to me?

Then there was a break. The wave slowed, and in slow motion, Fox reached for Gauder's telephone. It will not work. You can't reach anybody on this old telephone, in this goddamned telephone room, he thought. The wave ebbed. And in slow motion, he did reach Gauder's phone. It was hard to dial. First he got a wrong extension. Then, the next time, finally, he got outside the firm, and the number rang.

"Yes," Kim Hartman said. "Hello?"

What she heard was moaning, but she did not hang

up. She was not wrapped tight. She was very, very loose, and her mind was triggered by mystery and emotion.

"Fox?" she asked.

"Yes." It was all he could physically say because the wave came back, and took him. Kim waited. It was a long time before the wave went out to sea. Finally, Fox choked it out: "He got took."

He got took. All the deep places in Fox's childhood, arguments with his father that not even the best shrink could have ever gotten out of Fox. *They* swept through him. He said "took" like a little boy. It was what his father had told him when he was a little boy and his mother died: "She has been taken." Fox moaned. Oh Jesus, God. She got took. After the last telephone call. When he was a little boy. And from the telephone room he had talked to his mother while she was in the hospital, talked to her for the last time, and then never been connected with her again, no matter what number or operator he reached on the old phone.

"Oh, Robert. Where are you?"

"Gauder," Fox moaned.

"At his apartment?"

"No."

"You just stay there, Robert," Kim said. "Don't do anything, I'm just a cab ride away."

The building people took Gauder, quietly and easily, and probably without anyone else in the firm knowing about it, except two or three partners. Kim Hartman took Fox home, to the apartment that was now the Ardeonuig Hotel. She put him in bed, and made him a drink. She sat beside the bed, listening, waiting for the waves to pass. They were small waves now, little seizures. Sometimes he talked about his mother, and sometimes about his father, and sometimes about Gauder. It would have been confusing to a lot of people, but it wasn't to Kim Hartman. It was exactly the way she thought. And now, gradually, Fox became rational, drunk but occasionally making complete sense:

"We've got to get him into the *Times*," Fox said. He wanted more than a little notice inserted by the firm. He meant a nice little story. Here was a lawyer who had worked for so many years at the same law firm and had served on so many bar committees. They wouldn't, he thought, because Gauder had always handled things quietly, and never ever saw a policeman or had his picture in anything. "Oh, they won't," Fox said.

Now another small quake came, and he thought: And that's what will happen to me, just a little insert by the firm, as with Gauder, as with me, it will be a very small insert, not even containing "He leaves the loving widow and children." When he thought that, another small quake went through him.

"I don't have anyone," he said.

"Oh you do," she said. "Me. You've got me."

But Fox was still in the little tremor, and thinking of his mother, and said, "Nobody."

So she got in the bed with him, and leaned against the backboard, holding his head in her lap. He wanted himself listed under Gauder, loving son of, he thought then, but what good would it do? And he remembered how he had been listed under his father. And he thought, Yes, finally I'm glad.

"Fox," Kim Hartman said, "you've got me."

Did anyone have anybody?

"Fox," she said, "I do love you."

"I've got to stop," he said. "It's going to stop. It's ending."

"It doesn't matter if it stops. It's never going to stop, but you've got me, because I love you." Then she looked right down at him, her eyes fixed right at his, and Fox actually believed that she did love him. He actually accepted that fact, which he had never allowed himself before to accept from any other person, because he had believed deep in his heart that when you loved somebody, they got took, took like his mother, took as he had actually believed as a child: took away by his father.

"Oh Jesus," he moaned, "I'm sure glad you do."

41

"GOOD MORNING, basket case," Kim Hartman said. She brought in a breakfast tray and put it over Fox's stomach. Kim Hartman had style: it was even better service than at the Ardeonuig Hotel. Fox didn't know it, but he was getting the *New York Times,* the *Wall Street Journal,* and a rose, in addition to orange juice, Canadian bacon, and French toast made with rum.

"Are you going to take the sheet off your noggin?" she added. Fox wasn't sure. After having been wrapped tight for thirty-six years and suddenly unwrapping in one night, he just wasn't sure. He felt embarrassed, in some strange way, for having let his feelings go so far.

"Now listen, Fox," she said, "you've had an awful time, but you simply must come out from under that sheet."

She was right, he thought, I've got to go to the office. I've got to unwrap. So he pulled the sheet down. Kim Hartman was smiling at him. Fox almost cried, just because she looked so beautiful. Life is going to be a little different for me, he realized, but I'll get back to normal once I get back to the office.

"What time is it?" he asked.

"It doesn't matter what time it is," she answered. "And you're not going to the office. I called them and told them that you were sick. No more of this line of duty stuff, and how much you owe the firm because they made you a partner. Put things in perspective. You can take one day off."

She sounded exactly the way he had, talking to Jackson, but Fox didn't realize it. He didn't fully understand that he had been working through his problems all along. Using Jackson, or anything, to help him. *Could* he take a day off? That was what he was thinking. He had planned to see Banning today and finish with the whole Sifford affair. All right, he thought, Marsiglia said it had waited "thirteen damn years," it could wait one more day. And Marsiglia was very, very smart.

"Is it perfect?" Kim asked. "I wanted it to be exactly right." She was talking about the breakfast, and it was perfect. The fact that it was so perfect, and that she's wanted it to be, almost made Fox cry again. It was *definitely* not a day to go to the office, he realized.

"It's great," he said. But there now seemed to be a few new words in his briefcase brain, and he added, slowly, "It's wonderful, perfect. Thanks."

She sat down beside him on the bed.

"No, I made a mistake," she told him. "Yes, there is one mistake." And then she took both newspapers off the breakfast tray. "They don't allow newspapers at the Ardeonuig Hotel. That's something they do insist on. Seclusion from the outside world is the theme."

That's right, Fox thought, and they don't allow

newspapers at Broadmoor either. He started to eat his breakfast.

"How do you feel?" Kim Hartman asked Fox.

Fox felt as if there had been an earthquake and the bed was still shaking.

"Everything seems messed up. I feel like I made a fool of myself."

"That doesn't matter," Kim Hartman said. "Everything *is* all messed up and lost. Doormen don't open doors anymore. Railroads don't run on time. Conductors don't conduct. They don't say all aboard anymore. Everything needs rehabilitation. Even the train conductors. They sit around drinking beer. They ought to stand up straight and swing bronze lamps and yell all aboard that's coming aboard. But none of that matters."

"What does?"

"Fox, there is only one thing you have to understand. It doesn't matter that you lost your mother and grew up with your father. It doesn't matter that your father wasn't very good at talking to you. What matters is that they loved you. Do you understand?"

He didn't. Even though Fox's brains had been twisted, pulled, and mutilated, he didn't understand.

"Fox," Kim Hartman said, and now she had his head in her hands and was staring into his eyes. "Fox, listen to me. Your father loved you all right. If he hadn't, he would have sent you away. He would have given you up to one of those schools where they take the children at two. But he didn't. He didn't even think about giving you up until prep school. And even then, Fox, you came back to him. Fox, he loved you like mad. Fox, he loved you as much as Gauder did. More.''

Fox was crying. Not moaning, or sobbing, just crying: Silent tears were running down his face.

''Listen to me. Believe me. Believe this much: they both loved you as much as you loved them.''

Maybe it was Kim's hands. Who knows? Maybe even faith healing is possible. It is a very strange world.

''As much as I love you?'' Fox said. It took him a while, but he said it.

''Yes,'' Kim Hartman said. ''You understand.'' And she kissed him.

The law is a pessimist, assuming everyone will mess everything up. The lawyer works to clean up the messes people make. The law is stern, the way Fox's father had been. The law had been Fox's inheritance. Now, however, Fox suddenly felt a tingle of optimism. It was just there—deeply implanted in his brain.

Kim Hartman smiled. She looked for a second as if *she* was going to cry.

''It's really much easier to go to a shrink, Fox. It costs a lot of money, but it's easier, don't you think?''

''I don't know,'' Fox said deliberately.

''Well, it doesn't matter,'' Kim Hartman told him. ''I can see clearly that Foxes were not meant to go to shrinks. I'll never be able to get you even near one. I'm sure your father never even talked to anyone who had ever gone to a shrink. I forgive you your failings, Fox. I think I understand you. You know though, Fox, they even have shrinks who wear gray flannel suits, with offices on Wall Street. Can I get in bed with you?''

Of course she could. Why was she even bothering to ask? And then he realized it was because he would have to move the tray, which he did. She took off her robe, and slid in under the covers.

''I love spending the morning in bed,'' she said. ''And since neither of us is going to work, we could spend the entire day just talking and making love, with the phone off the hook. You would like that, wouldn't you?''

Like it? He would love it, but he wasn't sure he could do it. He was drained. So what happened was this: Kim Hartman held on to Fox, and after a while both of them fell asleep. And since she had taken the phone off the hook, nobody bothered them, and they did not wake up until late in the afternoon.

And when they did, Kim Hartman brought up the ''business'' about marriage, which is what she called it.

''Now, Fox, this business about marriage. I can't decide right now. It's all too emotional right now. But I want to tell you one thing, or sort of give you one thing.'' She paused. Shook her head. It was very hard for her to make up her mind about anything, and she paused as if she were having second thoughts.

''No, I'm right.'' She smiled, this time to herself, and then, to Fox. ''I will definitely live with you. Right here. You can move right in, and yes, give up your own apartment, I'm not going to back out on you. There is only one condition: you'll have to keep Robert at bay.''

"Which Robert?" Fox asked. There were, as Kim had said, too many Roberts in her life.

"My demented ex-husband, Robert Hartman. As soon as he learns that I'm living in sin, he's going to try to get custody of my son. He'll sue me for moral turpitude or something. You know what it is. He'll also want to stop paying me alimony. So, if I don't decide to marry you, and we end up living together endlessly, you will have to keep him at bay. If I do decide to marry you, Robert will be so happy about not paying alimony that he'll never bother me again. Is this all right, as a sort of interim agreement?''

"How long is interim?" Fox asked.

"Fox, it could be one day. It could be forty years. I never know when I'm going to make up my mind, or why. But my shrink taught me that it doesn't matter.''

She snuggled up to Fox. Fox had no trouble making up his mind: it didn't matter how long it took her. *He was moving in.*

42

Fox HAD NOT gone down easily. He had fought the ghosts of his father and mother to a standstill, and with the help of his life preserver, Kim Hartman, he was still on his feet. Functioning. And feeling better.

Two days ago, he had moved into Kim Hartman's apartment, instead of into Broadmoor. He had never really moved out of Kim's apartment, of course. But it took them two days to get some of Fox's furniture in.

Kim said that was important: Fox ought to have a study of his own, where he could hang his father's dusty diplomas and a picture of Gauder, and anything else he wanted. She also told him to put in his father's old bed: he had to have a place to sleep when they had fights and she locked him out of the bedroom. Kim Hartman understood that it was not "all over," for either herself or for Fox. "We're all doomed to spend the rest of our lives circling in the same stew with all the people we've touched, or been touched by," she said. "You don't get rid of them, even when they're dead."

Old Mrs. Sifford had never gotten rid of her husband. And Mrs. Banning was haunted now by the estate of Mrs. Sifford. Not quite a real person. But real enough to be represented by Fox.

Randolph opened the door and stood there, glaring at Fox. He's not the smiler today, Fox thought, has Mrs. Banning given him a dressing down?

"You were told not to come back," Randolph said. "But you have. Just like an old dog."

Randolph must have thought it was a very good joke. Now he smiled. The white teeth filling up the smile, smiling around clenched jaws.

"How does Mrs. Banning hold tea parties with you?" Fox asked politely.

"That's not the kind of party Mrs. Banning wants," Randolph said.

What does she want, Fox wondered, wakes? And then Fox thought of the mirrors Kim Hartman had kept because "they were sort of fun." How far had the lupus gone? What did Mrs. Banning enjoy? Or Randolph himself?

"Could you please step out of the way?" Fox said to the smiler.

Randolph actually did, and Fox went down the hall, and this time the flowers in the room were yellow. They were jonquils, a faded parchment yellow, creamy like the pages of a will. If I understood how she selects her flowers, I could guess her moods, Fox thought. Kim Hartman probably understands these things. Kim Hartman, who believed that one death always led to another, that ghosts followed everyone, had given Fox some advice because she had been scared. The advice was that people with quickly moving arthritis took a lot of pain killers. Pain killers do strange things to your mind.

"I let you in because you said this was going to be the last time we would have to talk," Mrs. Banning said. The aluminum walker was right in front of her. Her hands clenched it. Her face looked older than the parchment flowers. It was opaque white. Bulging veins thunked in her neck. Her chin stuck forward, the lower jaw out, her tongue at the corner of her mouth.

"I think it would be better if Randolph left," Fox said, looking past Mrs. Banning.

Randolph stood behind the sofa, arms crossed. In the white jacket, he looked like some kind of functionary.

"I don't," she said.

She snapped out her words. Well, she knows something is coming, probably knows exactly what it is, Fox thought. She is smart. And how crazy?

"You've made a lot of money with Marsiglia," Fox said. "You were very smart. I just want you to be smart again. It won't cost you much to give away three million or so dollars," Fox said slowly. "You're getting a deal."

"You must be mad," Banning said. "Everything you've ever said has been mad. Now get out."

"You took the money with Gladney," Fox said. Poor Gladney. He remembered that Gauder had said it was Gladney, but why had Gladney done it? How had he too been lured into the den of the wolf?

Gauder had guessed right: Mrs. Banning's hands

235

shook violently and the walker rattled. Good for Gauder.

"No," Mrs. Banning yelled, "I took no money."

"You walked into a strange bank, and pretended to be Mrs. Sifford. Frederick Gladney, her banker, vouched for you. You mortgaged the Meecham Building. And walked out with more than three million dollars. Which you invested with Marsiglia."

Fox was playing his hunches, trying to crack Mrs. Banning immediately.

"I can't even walk," she hissed.

"You could walk then," Fox said. "But tell me one thing, Mrs. Banning. Why did Frederick Gladney help you?"

Now the long chin poked forward, over the top of the walker, and her eyes betrayed a hint of the fatal seductress that had done in Charles Sifford, Sr., and who knows how many other men.

"Why do you think?" she hissed. "Randolph, he's trying to take my money. Kill him."

The blue veins were beating like worms on a hot plate. *"Kill him."*

"You've got plenty of money," Fox said calmly. He was looking at Randolph, and addressing words to him, not Mrs. Banning. Randolph was a smart boy. Fox had figured it out. The smart boy would decide to close the door of Mrs. Banning's cage. He would choose right now: from now on Randolph would handle Mrs. Banning's telephone, mail, and doorbell. And her money.

Mrs. Banning looked from Randolph to Fox and back again. She seemed to sense the doors being shut on her. Behind her walker, for an instant she looked like a trapped animal in a zoo.

"Kill him," Mrs. Banning barked. "He's trying to take the money. Shoot him."

"He's not going to kill me," Fox said, calmly looking to Randolph. "He doesn't want to go to jail."

But Randolph was still smiling. Being asked to kill Fox seemed to have put him in a good mood.

"Then give me the gun," Mrs. Banning yelled. Randolph just smiled.

"When you've thought it all through later, Mrs. Banning, you'll see that what I suggested is the only sensible thing to do. And you'll do it because you have no other choice."

Fox stood up. He didn't want to give Randolph any more time to think about where his best interests lay. And Mrs. Banning was getting up too. Apparently she was not going to think it through. She got up in her walker, and started across the room, her mouth open, like some shriveled, mummified ape, coming forward in her cage.

"Stop him, Randolph," she screamed. "Kill him, stop him."

"Be a good boy, Randolph," Fox said quietly, "and help Mrs. Banning, she's overly upset." Randolph just smiled. He seemed to enjoy seeing Mrs. Banning upset.

She was going to block off the hall if Fox didn't move, so he took his chances and walked slowly to the doorway. He had definitely cracked Banning.

Whack—the walker came down and Mrs. Banning took another small step at Fox. She was doing a tremendous amount of work, and slowly getting across the room. He started down the hall. *Whack.* And Mrs. Banning threw her walker in front of her, threw it too far, and tumbled down on the carpet. She knocked over the flowers as she went. And they covered her as if she were already dead. But she wasn't. Fox could hear her moaning.

"For Christ's sake," Fox said to Randolph, "give her some help."

Randolph finally did. He picked Mrs. Banning up and carried her over to the sofa, and dumped her down on it. And then Fox left, thinking: it's time. This has pushed her over the line, and now Randolph is in control, Mrs. Banning is truly in a cage. She'll be begging. Begging Randolph to take her to the bathroom. He'll monitor all her calls, so that she can't get rid of him. Randolph was smart enough not to kill me. He knows where his best interests lie, even if Mrs. Banning does not.

43

FOX WENT straight to Gladney's office. Banning had thrown a scare into him. He didn't want Gladney to do something stupid, like jump out the window. Fox also thought that the whole affair would work better in Gladney's office—with his job, and the importance of it, surrounding Gladney. Fox could threaten just to walk upstairs, with the papers Marsiglia had given him, and have Gladney terminated right then and there. There were a lot of ways he could play it, but all his careful planning momentarily slipped his mind when he saw Gladney's office.

The construction men had reached the thirteenth floor. Gladney, dressed in his dark blue double-breasted old-fashioned suit, with his little tortoiseshell half glasses, and his prep school accent, was now surrounded by shining stainless steel, black Formica, and all the other things that went with "macho banking."

"I don't know if I can talk, Fox," Gladney said. "I am not even sure that I want to."

The few papers on Gladney's desk were in total disarray, forming a kind of modern art geometric design. The big shining steel and smoked-glass desk seemed to overwhelm him. He sort of cowered behind it.

"I tried to threaten them," he said. "I explained that a trust department must have a certain elan, but they don't care. 'Macho banking.' 'Cojones.' Up theirs, I say. But it's good to see you, Fox, to see someone who hasn't changed, and won't."

But Fox had changed.

"Frederick, I want to talk to you about Mrs. Sifford, Mrs. Banning, and three million dollars."

"I can't talk, Fox. I can't think straight in this cold, cruel office they've built around me."

"What I'm going to talk about will take your mind off the decor." Fox looked at Gladney's windows. Now they were lined with steel trim, and there didn't seem to be any way to open them. Good, Fox thought, he won't be able to jump.

"What?"

"You're my friend," Fox said quietly. "So I want you to listen carefully and trust me. If you do, you can stay on and get your gold watch."

"Are you crazy, Fox?"

"I know all about Mrs. Banning and you, and how you got Mrs. Sifford's money. I can even prove it, if I have to. I don't want to, though, and I don't think I need to."

"You've gotten confused, Fox," Gladney said.

"Nothing's confused."

"I don't have any money."

"Because Mrs. Banning signed the papers. You vouched for her. Why?"

"*I* didn't sign anything."

He won't crack, Fox thought. I'm trying to save him, and he won't crack.

"Listen, you vouched for the fact that Mrs. Sifford

would arrive at a certain bank to take out a mortgage. Mrs. Banning arrived instead. Then she signed the papers. She had the poor drunk son cosign them as well. Then she marched back to the bank, or mailed them in. It doesn't matter. I know all that. You know it too. I'm trying to give you a break. I'm just asking you to make a couple of phone calls, so that I don't have to march upstairs."

"Upstairs?"

"Up to your president's office, Frederick. The one with cojones. The one who's going to fire you, and put you in jail. The macho banker."

Gladney cracked. Fox could see it physically. The old banker slouched down in his chair, his eyes staring up as if the cut-glass chandelier in the dining room were twirling above him in this office.

"Why did you do it?"

"I don't know."

"She blackmailed you?"

"No, Fox, this was the only thing I did wrong."

"What?"

Gladney's eyes suddenly bore down on Fox. They looked red, jiggling, like the eyes of Martin Beard. "How the hell can I explain it to you? Thirteen years ago, I was in love with Cora Banning. She fucked me, Fox, and then she fucked me over. You want the truth? You have it. And I never even got a cent. Banning double-crossed me and took it all. What more do I have to say?"

Fox sat alone in the musty trophy room of the Trout Club, drinking a Scotch. The mounted and stuffed fish that lined the walls seemed to stare down with the eyes of Frederick Gladney. You could not get the deadness out of the fish eyes, even if you put in fake glass ones. There was a sadness to these stuffed fish, and a sadness to Frederick Gladney, who had been caught, stuffed, and now probably would be better off dead, nailed to an ironing board and mounted here at the Trout Club, with a plaque saying: Sucker Fish. Caught by Mrs. Cora Banning. Taken by Mrs. Banning thirteen years ago with little or no fight. Weight: about one sixty pounds. Length: six feet or so. Big old sucker fish, taken by the bare hands, a rod being unnecessary in the big river called New York.

Gladney had vouched for Mrs. Banning. He had made the necessary telephone calls. Then Mrs. Banning had arrived at the bank, and, pretending to be Mrs. Sifford, had mortgaged the Meecham Building. It was a perfect crime. Who ever bothered to check the dusty records in the New York office where the deeds were recorded? Who would know? All this happened three days before Mrs. Sifford caught Banning with her husband.

Another sucker fish, Fox thought, taken by Mrs. Banning. Plucked from the polluted river. Maybe Mr. Sifford ought to be dug up too, and hung on the wall alongside Gladney. Banning wanted it all. Money and revenge too. Too many insults. Mount Mrs. Sifford on the wall too. Hang them all up on the wall together. Mrs. Banning was quite a fisherwoman. Big fish too.

The plan had been that Gladney and Banning would make the interest payments regularly, to insure that no one would find out about the loan. After all, how long could Mrs. Sifford live? When she died, the estate would have to pay off the mortgage. They would just blame it all on the eccentricities of Mrs. Sifford. There had been another part of the plan: Banning would leave town. Gladney would take early retirement and join her. Only Mrs. Banning hadn't run anywhere except to the Blagden Building.

So who had paid the interest on the mortgage? Gladney himself. Selling his old inherited house and land. Selling it in the end for interest payments that in thirteen years had amounted to more than three million dollars. He had done it to protect his reputation. What else did he have left? He was a double-crossed sucker fish. No, he hadn't signed anything. That was true. Mrs. Banning had the check, the three million. All Gladney had was the guilt. Go ahead, turn me in, Banning had dared him. He hadn't dared.

"It was the only thing I've done wrong, Fox," Gladney had whined. And Fox had told Gladney that he could stay on at the bank, and get his gold watch, but on the condition that he helped crack Banning and get the money back. Gladney was to send her a letter, with a copy to Fox, confessing to everything. If that didn't crack Banning, Gladney would send another letter, this time to Randolph. Randolph would understand. And force Banning to spit out the money. After all, there would be plenty left, plenty for Randolph and Mrs. Banning to play with.

"Do you want another drink, Mr. Fox?"

Fox looked at the old waiter. He hadn't heard him come in. Probably an old fisherman. Used to quietly sneaking up on the fish.

"Yes. Thank you."

And I'm a fish too, we are all fish. And sooner or

later we get caught and mounted on the wall of the Trout Club. Even if it's not by Banning. You still get taken. Fox looked at the rows of fish. How many of them had old Gauder taken? Quite a few. He had been some fisherman. And Fox's own father had taken some of the big ones that lined the walls of the trophy room of the Trout Club. But not me, Fox thought. I use barbless hooks and throw all the fish back. I let them swim away. Is it right?

Was it? Was it right to let Frederick Gladney stay on at the bank, keep swimming in the big river. He had lied once, cheated once. Swindled and been swindled in return by the master fisherwoman, Banning. He might do it again. Was it right to throw him back?

You could not get the deadness out of the eyes of these fish, Fox thought, looking at a huge brown trout that, in the shadows, looked sad and very, very dead. And that was what bothered Fox. Deadness of any kind. In fish, in people. So he had to throw them back. He was not Banning, or even Marsiglia, or the old Baron Meecham. What had the nurse wife said? "I only care about people, Mr. Fox."

"Your drink, sir. Would you like me to turn on the lights?"

It was the waiter, back with the Scotch.

"No," Fox said, "but thank you."

"You really can't see the trophy fish in the dark, Mr. Fox."

"I really don't want to."

Even in the dark, he could clearly see the glass eyes of death staring down at him reproachfully. Why do I throw them back? Why do I let them live? It is because I believe, in some mystical way, as mystical as anything that Kim Hartman believes, that the time I give to the fish, even to the big sucker fish like Gladney, will be added to my own life time. Fox pondered: I let them all live because, essentially, I'm scared of getting nailed to the wall.

44

IT TOOK two letters from Gladney, with copies to Fox, before Randolph telephoned.

"I have something for you," Randolph said.

In the background, Fox heard a hissing, slow-motion sound: Mrs. Banning's breathing.

"Good," Fox said. "Bring it down to my office."

"You say you won't come to the apartment?"

The hissing breathing sound got louder: Fox imagined Banning on the sofa, hunched down behind her walker, breathing through her teeth. "Won't come to the apartment?" Very interesting, Fox thought. Randolph is giving me some kind of message.

"No," Fox said. "I definitely will not come to the apartment. You come here."

"Mr. Savile is waiting for you, sir," Miss Algur said from the door.

Sir? Fox thought that was a little much. He didn't recognize that Algur regarded his transformation from lunatic lawyer to unzipped partially functioning person as an example of divine intervention.

"Who?" Fox said.

"Randolph Savile," she said.

Savile? Interesting, Fox thought. Why didn't he choose a name like Mr. St.-Tropez, or Mr. Bermuda?

And then Fox understood: Randolph, standing in the door, had new clothes. The double-breasted suit was pinched at the waist. His hair was greased and shone. The silk tie bulged out: Savile Row.

"Sit down, Randolph," Fox said, "and while you're at it, what is your real name anyway?"

"None of your business," Randolph said.

"I don't think there should be any secrets between us," Fox said loosely. "I'm not going to tell anyone. I'm just curious, that's all."

"Sarraille," Randolph said. "So what?"

"No so what," Fox said. "They're both good names."

Would Fluffy Ravenel meet Mr. Savile in some bar? What would she think of him if she did? Fox wondered. Not much. Poor Randolph, Fox thought, you can't change your name and change yourself. A little shiver ran through him: he had changed his name. There was no Robert Fox, *Jr.*, on the letterhead of Castle and Lovett. There never had been. His father had died just before Fox had been made partner. As an associate, he had been Fox, Jr. As a partner, he was plain Fox. My father never got to see me make partner, Fox thought. And a small wave hit him. But it doesn't matter, he told himself. He loved me.

"How is Mrs. Banning?"

Randolph crossed his legs, and lit a cigarette. The smoke seemed as white as his teeth. Fox kicked his wastebasket toward Randolph so the ashes would have somewhere to fall.

"Wadda you expect?" Mr. Randolph Savile said. "She's at home."

"And how does she spend her time?"

"Hating you," Randolph snapped. "I thought I was just here to deliver the money. Not to chat."

But he wants to talk, Fox thought: Otherwise, he would not have lit the cigarette. He wants to tell me something.

"Hating me, Randolph?"

"I'm not supposed to give you any money," Randolph said. "You know what I'm supposed to do?"

"What?" Fox asked.

"Use this."

Randolph reached down into the pockets of his beautiful suit: what came out was small and had a handle the color of Randolph's teeth. It was a gun.

"Put it away," Fox said. "Better yet, throw it out."

"I can't," Randolph said. "I need it."

And then Fox realized what Randolph was trying to tell him, and why Randolph had lit the cigarette: Randolph was scared. Maybe all zookeepers are, Fox thought. You bring the wolf his meat. He's dozing in the corner. His eyes are closed. The long lashes interlock. Can you really see his eyes behind them? Is he sleeping? Are the muscles really relaxed? Is the wolf waiting, waiting to jump you?

"There's an alternative," Fox said. "She can be institutionalized."

"What is that?"

"She can be put away. Does she have any family?"

"No," Randolph said. "She is alone."

A lone wolf, Fox thought.

"You're smart," he said. "Let's think together, Randolph. What can be done?"

Randolph sat there smoking. You could not tell if he was thinking or not. What kind of a woman was Mrs. Banning? Fox wondered.

"She wants to screw everybody," Randolph said nonchalantly. "That's all I know."

Screw everybody. Yes, yes, Fox thought. I suppose Randolph is using that old Southern saying. She "screwed" Gladney and pretended she was a pathetic little woman, and led Gladney on. Then cut him off at the knees. A very interesting woman. But as Kim Hartman says, it all comes back to haunt you.

"I've got her under control," Randolph added, "and I've got this." He patted his pocket. "If we put her in the bin, then I don't get any money. Unless I can find a smart lawyer. You know what I mean?"

Fox knew exactly what Randolph meant: he, Fox, was supposed to lie and cheat. So that Randolph "Savile" could end up with Mrs. Banning's money, and Mrs. Banning could end up at Broadmoor.

"I understand completely," Fox said. Except it just was not done. Gauder would not have done it, Fox thought. And neither would my father. Mrs. Banning definitely belongs in Broadmoor, he thought. And Randolph? A small pension would do. He could work as a waiter and try to get a job in show business. It was just one more problem. But not too large. Randolph was in too deep. He thought he had control, but he didn't. The gun didn't do anything for him. Randolph would have to sign a deposition declaring that Mrs. Banning was insane. Her money would go into a trust to keep her in Broadmoor. What could Randolph do about it? But all this would take some time.

"Randolph, I take it that for the time being you have the situation under control."

Fox got that big, ugly smile.

"You mean do I have her tied down or something, so that she won't murder you?"

"I mean are you both all right?"

"For the time being," Randolph said. "Right now, she's just angry at you. That's all right."

Not exactly, Fox thought, but it will have to do. For the time being. He didn't like the gun. He didn't like Mrs. Banning. And Mr. Savile?

"Randolph, leave the gun here."

"No," Randolph said. "She would know."

"Know what?"

"Know that I'm not going to kill you," Randolph said. "That's how I keep her under control."

Interesting, Fox thought. Maybe Randolph Savile wasn't so bad after all. And I had thought he would tie her to the bed and make her beg. Maybe we won't have to institutionalize her after all. Maybe she'll just have to go to the hospital when the disease finishes her.

"All right, Randolph," Fox said, standing up. "Now for the check."

It was as if Randolph really didn't want to turn over the envelope. It was cream white. Fox took it from Randolph and opened it. Inside there was a certified check for three million two hundred thousand dollars, made out to the Estate of Mrs. Belinda Meecham Sifford. Fox's *particular three million two*.

"I take it this is really her signature," Fox said.

"I was a good messenger boy," Randolph said, and he stood up too. "I promised to shoot you right here in your office, and she signed it."

"What will you tell her now?"

"That there were guards. Or that I discovered a better way to do it. I'm good at lying."

He bent down and stubbed out his cigarette on the side of the wastebasket.

Good at lying? Fox thought. So was Mrs. Banning. Very, very good. And very, very smart and very dangerous. She has to go to Broadmoor, Fox thought. No matter how well Randolph is taking care of her

45

EVERYTHING SEEMED quiet now. There are times at law firms when all is spinning and unraveling, and other times when the most interesting thing happening is the breakdown of a typewriter.

Jackson came in and sat down without being asked to. Everything was slightly better now, even Jackson. Or did I *make* him always ask if he could sit? Fox wondered.

"What can I do for you?" Fox asked.

"The loan isn't clear to me," Jackson said. "That was one of the things I wanted to ask. You say the three million and change was a long-term loan from Mrs. Sifford to Mrs. Banning? How can that be?"

Things are apparently too quiet, Fox thought. I've got to get Jackson some interesting work. The Sifford matter was almost wrapped up. There was just the art stuff to go. And putting Mrs. Banning in Broadmoor with Martin Beard.

Fox had thought through the various ways to "adjust" the "funds," and decided a long-term, no-interest loan from generous old Mrs. Sifford to her friend, confidante, and personal secretary, Mrs. Banning, was the most sensible way.

"I know," Fox said. "It's a little strange. But anything can happen with these old battle-axes. Call it a loan."

"Come on," Jackson said, "it's important that I know."

"Why?"

"I'm getting to that," Jackson told him. "There's another thing. The advertisements. Why are we advertising for Mr. Sifford in places like the Fairbanks, Alaska, *Gazette?* Why no ads here in the *Times?* And why are the notices so small?"

Jackson was talking about the notices that Fox was required by law to insert in newspapers of general circulation, seeking the whereabouts of old missing Mr. Sifford. He had a good answer for Jackson on that, and it was almost, but not quite, the complete truth.

"Jackson, there are too many lunatics in New York City. If we advertise in the *Times,* we'll have a thousand Martin Beards stumbling in here, drunk out of their skulls, and messing things up. You want more Martin Beards?"

"No," Jackson said, "but there's got to be more to it than that."

"Maybe a little more," Fox said. "But you know most of it."

Even though Fox hadn't advertised in the *New York Times,* there appeared to be some strange network among the crazies and mumblers of New York City. Already, several had, like Martin Beard, come into the office, their coats tattered, red eyes blazing, shaking old papers. He had talked to some of them.

Some he'd turned over to Jackson. You had to give them something, or they kept coming back.

"Anything else?" Fox asked. "It's a slow day. I've got no desire to deal with sub-chapter S corporations. What's new, Jackson?"

Jackson rubbed his hand across his mouth. Then across his forehead.

"There is something, isn't there?" Fox said.

"Yes, there is. I just don't know quite how to say it. And, look, you could give me some advice, too. I want you to know I haven't actually done anything yet."

"I understand," Fox said seriously. He did: when young associates talked this way, it was because they had had an offer.

"Who gave it to you?" Fox asked.

"Lambert. In Houston. And it includes a car, a salary increase, and a guaranteed partnership within two years. In writing. Can you give me that?"

Could he? Fox wondered. How much power did he have? He wasn't Richard Lovett, jetting around the country with the senior partners of investment banking houses. You can't lie, Fox thought.

"No," he said slowly. "I can't guarantee it. There are just too many smart boys, and they all want to be partner, and you know all about that. You came at a bad time, Jackson. When I started it was a much smaller firm, and in general, if you could tie your tie and keep your shoes on, you would make partner. But New York has changed. So has the firm. I wish I could."

"You do?" Jackson said.

"Sure. You're very good. And I could atone for the hell I put you through."

Now Jackson was rubbing his temples. It was a hard choice.

So Texas firms were offering cars to lure the smart young lawyers out of New York. All we give them is money, Fox thought, but we do give them a lot of it. I guess we'll have to start giving them even more. Ther are too many bright boys now. Of course, things could change if they all go to Texas. At least we'll have something interesting to talk about at the next partnership meeting.

"What kind of a car is it?" Fox asked.

"It doesn't matter," Jackson said. "I don't even know. I buy it. They give an allowance for it. I don' care about the car, but it would be nice to know you'll make partner."

"How do you like New York?" Fox asked.

"I'm not sure about that either."

Who is? Fox wondered.

"And you don't know how you'll like Texas, so you really are stuck. Right?"

"This partnership part of it," Jackson said. "Guar anteed. In writing. I don't care about the money."

"I didn't think you did," Fox said, "but I'm willing to try to bribe you by offering a whopping salary increase if you stay. As I said, you're very good. But I know what you mean. It is a lot nicer to make partner than not to make partner."

And then he thought of Jackson's stomach. Coulc the guy last for seven more years in New York wondering each day whether he was going to make t?

"Jackson, go to Houston," Fox said.

"Why?" Jackson said. "Tell me why."

"You asked my advice. You're good all right, but t's costing you a lot to be perfect. The nice thing about being a partner is that you don't have to be perfect anymore. It's more than power. So go to Houston. And I'll throw in an escape clause: you can come back here if you don't like it there. How is hat?"

"Pretty good," Jackson said.

"Then why do you look so damn serious?" Fox asked.

"I've enjoyed working with you," Jackson said solemnly.

"Come on, Jackson," Fox said. "Let's not try to id ourselves."

Now Jackson *did* stop frowning.

"At least it was sort of interesting," he said. "Weird, but interesting."

"That's more like it," Fox said.

"I mean, ambulances?"

"Jackson, that doesn't happen all the time. Honestly, his firm is very stodgy, and only once in a while do we deal with lunatics. We just take it as it comes. Listen, about the party . . ."

Jackson interrupted. "What party?"

"You get a party, if you want one, when you leave. The firm gives you one if you're not made partner, and have to leave. In your case, it's usually, well, your kind of party is supposed to be held by our peers, not the firm. So tell the other associates when they give you your party that Mr. Fox would like to attend. All right?"

"Sure," Jackson said. He apparently wanted to do something because he had walked over to Fox's desk.

"No, Jackson, we don't shake hands now," he told him. "That comes on the day you do, in fact, leave the firm. Then I stand up, too, and tell you how good you've been all over again, and we shake. Say in about a month?"

"A month?" Jackson said. "Why?"

"Well, you do expect a good letter of recommendation to carry around with you, don't you?" Fox said. "So I expect you to finish all your present assignments, including the Sifford matter, and leave everything nice and tidy when you go. If they're willing to throw in the car, they'll be willing to wait. Got it?"

Jackson shook his head. Was it worth it?

"All right," he said finally. "Thanks for the advice. I'll stay a month."

Fox had changed, and yes, he was not so tightly wrapped, but of course, after a catharsis, one has a tendency to regress.

46

THERE WAS going to be an auction. The appraised value of the art in Mrs. Sifford's town house came to approximately nine million five. Things had changed in the art world, Kim Hartman said. Ten years ago, the big Church painting of the surging sunlight, with the four mountains of the Hudson River and the old Sifford Mansion in it, was worth, perhaps, one hundred thousand dollars. Now, American art was very popular. That one painting alone was worth approximately seven hundred and fifty thousand dollars.

That fact was sort of interesting, because, in terms of real value, that was about what the painting had cost old Baron Meecham when he had purchased it a hundred years ago. Which is why Frederick Church was able to build his own big mansion on the Hudson River, and also rent a steamer when he wanted to go out and paint icebergs.

Icebergs had been Frederick Church's passion, the way railroad building had been Meecham's. All this is true, Fox thought. Anything can happen in New York. Fox was staring at the big painting and the four huge mountains. The auction was going to be held in the Sifford town house itself. Kim Hartman had sort of rearranged things, moving paintings into special rooms, so that they would complement each other and increase the buying frenzy. They are going to grab at this stuff like spawning trout, Kim Hartman had told Fox. He was rubbing off on her. It was so agreeable to live with Kim Hartman and to be around her that Fox visited the town house all the time. They had even, once, gone for it in old Mrs. Sifford's bed, the one she had refused to sleep in. As Kim Hartman said, it didn't matter, because the guard Fox had gotten to replace the thug that butchered Martin Beard was about eighty and slept all day.

Whack! And then a sliding sound coming from the hall.

Fox should have heard it, but he didn't. It was a soft whack, and both Fluffy Ravenel and Kim Hartman were babbling. Jackson was also talking: he was at the town house too, saying good-bye to Fluffy.

Whack, whack, it came each time. Then the sliding.

"Houston?" Fluffy said to Jackson, "Ah *love* Houston. You mean I'll have someone to play with in Houston?"

Play with? Fox thought. What a mind.

"You know, the art world is busting out in Houston," Fluffy babbled on to Jackson. "I tell you a lot of this stuff is going to end up there."

"Why don't you come down and appraise it?" Jackson asked. He could hardly keep his eyes off Fluffy.

Yes, Fox thought, it all comes back to haunt you.

Jackson may get a chance to look at this Sifford stuff when he goes to the Houston Museum of Fine Arts. Will it remind him of Martin Beard?

Whack, whack, whack.

Kim Hartman was trying out a little Church painting over the mantelpiece. It was a study of icebergs. She hung it, and then stepped back.

"What do you think?" she said.

"I think it's just fantastic," Fluffy said. "I don't know how you do it. It's perfect. Just where it ought to be. What do you say?"

She was talking to Jackson.

"I don't know anything about art," Jackson said.

"Would you go for it?" Fluffy prodded Jackson.

Fox snapped around. In his mind that meant only one thing, but he would have to learn to remember that it could be used in many different contexts.

"It looks good there," Jackson muttered.

"I think so too," Kim Hartman said.

"You do know about art," Fluffy said to Jackson. "You see. You have the instinct."

Interesting, Fox thought, now that Jackson has taken some definitive step, is moving to Houston, Fluffy really seems to like him. Or at least to appreciate him. When he's gone, I will miss him too.

As usual, Kim Hartman changed her mind.

"I don't know," she said. "Maybe it would be better in the hall. It's only two fifty." She was talking thousands, of course.

"But this is the Church room," Fluffy said.

259

"It might sort of whet their appetites if they saw a tiny jewel out there," Kim said. "I want them crazed when they get in here. In a frenzied, buying mood."

Whack, whack, whack. Fox still didn't hear it. It was interesting how Kim had set this whole thing up. The penthouse apartment was where all the modern art was going to be shown. It had turned out that Mrs. Sifford had a lot of it. Stored in the basement. No skeletons down there, just modern paintings, by people like Stella, de Kooning. Fox couldn't remember the names. He really liked this Church painting, though, the one of the mountains. It made him wish he had seven fifty to buy it. But not enough to go out and steal for it.

Whack.

He heard it because his mind had gradually hit on the word steal, and for an instant he froze. *Whack.* He heard it too late. Mrs. Banning stood at the doorway in her walker. *Keys,* Fox thought, goddamn it *keys.* She had a key, like Martin Beard. Perfect Jackson, blown out by Fluffy Ravenel, had forgotten to change the locks. Or did I forget to tell him?

"You took my money," Banning screamed.

Fluffy and Kim Hartman jerked around. Jackson stood like a statue: frozen, perfect. Another work of art. Where the hell is the guard? Fox thought. This is his job. And how did she get out of the apartment? Crazy and smart, he thought. Zookeeper Randolph lost his beast. And why the hell did Algur tell her where I was?

"Good morning, Mrs. Banning," Fox said slowly and quietly.

She had one hand on the walker. She looked like the figurehead on the prow of some sailing vessel, a ghost ship, that had been out to sea too long, the paint peeled off, the wood bleached white, and twisted slightly by the long time at sea. Fox took a step forward, toward her.

"You filth," Mrs. Banning shouted.

She had something in her hand. For a second, Fox thought it was a piece of jewelry. And then he thought, she's going to throw something at me, and finally, his mind snapped in place and he realized that although it was very small and silvery, it was not jewelry at all. It was the gun and she was going to kill him with it.

One hand on the walker, the other with the little gun. Her hand shaking from the arthritis, but now pointing more or less at Fox: she shot. There was a little popping sound. And the shaking hand sent a bullet into the Church painting, right into the mountains.

"Fox!" Kim Hartman screamed. *"Move!"*

Why didn't he? Because it was all happening too fast and his mind could not take it all in. She is definitely going to Broadmoor, Fox thought, not back to that apartment. And she's going straight from here.

"Move! Move!" Kim screamed.

The white hand jigged a lot, but Mrs. Banning could still pull a trigger. This time the soft pop sent a bullet into the wall.

"Move, oh Jesus Christ, please. Move! Run!" Kim Hartman screamed.

Fluffy Ravenel moved instead: it had taken her a little time to dig down into her purse, dig down through the makeup, the address book that was so important to her, and the appointment calendar that was all booked up, and then a little more time for her to get into position the way her daddy had taught her, both hands on her gun and in a semisquat, but she was a fast girl, and smart, and before Mrs. Banning had gotten off the third shot, Fluffy Ravenel had placed a slug in Banning's chest that blew her backward, her hand still holding the walker, a slug that hit her with such force that she was thrown out into the hall.

I blew it, Fox thought. For the first time, there are going to be police. That was what he actually thought. He had never even considered the fact that he might be killed. He had not been trained for that. And there hadn't been time to think. And besides, he felt protected by some special god, living with Kim in the Ardeonuig apartment.

He looked at the doorway leading to the hall. What he saw was the aluminum cage, still in the doorway, and just Mrs. Banning's hand, still gripping it, still clenched, and now, finally in the spasm of death, shaking like a rattle, the aluminum shaking too, a rattling fierce sound that now, suddenly, scared the complete hell out of Fox.

47

THE POLICE DID come, but so did Marsiglia, after Fox's telephone call, so Fluffy Ravenel never did get her picture on the front page of the *New York Times*. At the auction, Marsiglia bought the picture of the mountains and the old Sifford house. He did care about art, and didn't give a damn that it had a hole in it. He just had it restored. The auction wasn't as big a success as it would have been if Fluffy had been on the front page of the *Times,* but everything sold anyway. Kim Hartman had them in a frenzy by the time they got into the room with all the Churches. It was easy for her: she was crazed herself by the time she got to the Church room. And craziness is contagious. Kim Hartman believed that it all came back to haunt you. A part of Mrs. Banning had to be in that room, watching the gavel come down. Kim Hartman was so nervous that she used her pearls as prayer beads.

"I was sure you were going to get killed," Kim Hartman said the night after Mrs. Banning died. "Just when everything is going very, very well, they take it all away from you."

"Who are 'they'?" Fox asked. *They* were lying in bed.

"Everyone," Kim Hartman said. "I don't know. It doesn't matter."

Some mind, Fox thought, she believes in ghosts.

"I can't sleep," she added. "I'm not going to sleep tonight."

Then she pushed herself down in the bed, and put her head on Fox's chest and her hands on his shoulders.

"I'm going to think of you as a surfboard," she said. "And pretend that I'm riding a big green wave toward some sandy beach. Maybe that will put me to sleep."

Surfboard? Fox thought. Fluffy Ravenel had gunned down Mrs. Banning, and Kim Hartman thinks about surfboards.

"Have you ever surfed?" Fox asked. He had never even *seen* a surfboard.

"I've done everything at least once. I've even been to a tennis camp, and I still can't play," Kim Hartman said. "That's the trouble. And it all comes back."

Well, Banning won't, Fox thought.

"I've done everything once, and I've always done it wrong," Kim Hartman said, surfing on Fox. "You didn't move," she said. "You didn't run. So I knew you were going to get took, Fox. You know what I thought?"

"No," Fox said.

"I thought about myself, not you. I thought: Now I'm not going to have him. I get lucky, and then he's gone. You know what I mean?"

And surprisingly, Fox did know what she meant. People do learn things. He had gone a long way, but not in a complete circle. He was not back where he had started. He knew just what she meant: she meant she loved him.

"I feel like I own New York," Fox said.

"Nobody owns anything anymore," Kim Hartman answered.

BOOKS BY
JOHN JAY OSBORN, JR.

__THE PAPER CHASE

(A31-141, $2.95, U.S.A
(A31-142, $3.75, Canad⬩

The novel that started it all. This is the nove
written by a Harvard Law School student that se
off one of the most stirring success stories of ou
time. As a book, it was tremendously acclaimed
As a movie, it became a legend. Now you ca
meet Professor Kingsfield, in all his icy em
nence, and his students, in all their swiftl
vanishing innocence, as they play out a drama ⬩
education in far more than the law, a drama tha
will enthrall you from first page to last.

__THE MAN WHO OWNED NEW YORK

(B31-260, $3.50, U.S.A
(B31-261, $4.50, Canad⬩

A graduate of Harvard College and Harvard La
School, John Jay Osborn, Jr. has clerked for
Federal Circuit Judge, worked in a Wall Stre⬩
law firm, and is now a law professor. Now, afte
the success of THE PAPER CHASE, he ha
written a novel of money, murder an
love . . . and a Wall Street lawyer determined ⬩
learn the truth about them all.

Don't Miss These Other Great Books By P. D. JAMES!